Spellcasters

CRYSTAL SUNG

ILLUSTRATED BY WENDY TAN

CHAPTER ONE

The aroma of frying garlic, onions and ginger filled the kitchen. Pots bubbled and sizzled on the hob as Jenny's grandparents darted around, stirring, sprinkling, adding pinches of this and that.

Por Por smacked a warm, grandmotherly kiss on Jenny's cheek

as she sat down for breakfast. "My darling *bao-beh*'s first day at secondary school."

"Yeah, and if my new passport hadn't taken so long to arrive, I could have started two weeks ago with everyone else," Jenny said. "They'll all have made friends already."

"Don't you worry; you'll find your way." Gong Gong bounced over, waving a pair of chopsticks. "We're packing your favourite dishes for lunch to keep you going." Jenny's grandfather plopped plump meatballs into a pan of bubbling oil.

Her grandparents were acting like

it was her first day at school *ever*! Jenny had lived all over the world with her parents, going wherever the next big job was. Her mum was an environmental scientist and her dad was a photographer. It sounded glamorous, but she'd lost count of the number of schools she'd been to, and starting over each time was hard. That's why Jenny had begged her parents to let her stay with Por Por and Gong Gong, so she could go to a secondary school in the UK while they finished their latest project in Thailand. It was Jenny's chance to put down some roots and get past the "new girl" stage for once.

Gong Gong lifted a rattling lid, releasing a cloud of steam. "You want a *lin yong bao*? Fresh and hot." He handed Jenny a plate with a white bun on it.

"Mmm, thanks!" Jenny took a bite and sweet lotus paste filled her mouth. The butterflies in her stomach settled. Gong and Por's cooking was the best.

"I can't believe you're starting at Spellcroft High today!" Aunty Connie whirled into the kitchen in a flowing tangerine maxi dress. "Feels like you were in nappies only last week! Mmm, that for me?" She ducked down and took a bite of Jenny's *bao*.

"Hey, get your own!" Jenny snatched her *bao* back, grinning.

Gong Gong chuckled and handed Aunty Connie her own *bao*.

"Red bean soup?" Por Por ladled the sweet soup into bowls and drizzled some creamy coconut on top.

"Thank you for the special breakfast and packed lunch." Jenny sipped the soup, the liquid warming her from the inside. "But you didn't have to go to so much trouble."

"Yes, they did – you know what they're like, Jenny," said Aunty Connie warmly.

Por Por put a lid on the soup pot and

sat down at the table. "We promised your mum and dad we'd take good care of you, *bao-beh*."

Jenny had spoken to her parents on a video call the night before. They were at an elephant sanctuary in Chiang Mai, where Mum was working on a research project about baby elephants. Dad had taken some brilliant photographs – elephant calves were so cute! The connection wasn't great though, and they kept freezing. Jenny was used to being away from home, but this was her first time away from Mum and Dad. It felt a bit weird.

Por Por patted Jenny's arm, her eyes

twinkling behind her glasses. "I have a surprise for you." She handed Jenny a small red velvet pouch.

"Wow, thanks!" Jenny loosened the drawstring and tipped out something heavy. It was a smooth, round bracelet made from jadeite. "It's gorgeous!" Jenny slid the bracelet on to her wrist. The jade stone felt lovely and cool on her skin.

"This bracelet belonged to my mother – your great-grandmother, Tai Por. In each generation of our family, it has been passed down to the eldest daughter. Your mother wanted you to have it to mark your first day of

secondary school. You are growing up,
bao-beh!" Por Por sniffed.

"It's your good luck charm," said
Aunty Connie with a smile. "Just like
my necklace." She tapped the pear-
shaped jade pendant hanging on a gold

chain around her neck.

Por Por squeezed Jenny's shoulders. "Spellcroft is going to be a great new start for you."

After breakfast, Jenny brushed her teeth and put on her shoes and new school blazer. It was navy to match her skirt, and on the front pocket was the Spellcroft High badge, embroidered with an oak tree.

Gong Gong heaved Jenny's bag on to her back. With all the lunch and snacks, it weighed a ton.

"So grown up." Por Por hugged her,

blinking hard. "Bye bye, *bao-beh*."

"Have a good day, *sayang*." Gong Gong hugged her too.

Jenny and Aunty Connie waved goodbye and stepped out on to Spellcroft Street.

It was warm for a September morning and the traders setting up for the market were still in shorts and T-shirts. Jenny and Aunty Connie walked past stalls bursting with fruits and vegetables, tables stacked with flowing *salwar kameez*, and stands crammed with shiny pots and pans for sale. Aunty Connie seemed to know everyone at the market.

"All right, Connie?" one stallholder called out.

"I'm good, thanks!" she replied.

At the end of the street they came to The Oaks – the community centre where Jenny's aunt worked.

"Do you remember coming here when you visited with your mum and dad?" asked Aunty Connie, stopping outside the building.

Jenny glimpsed leafy treetops stretching up behind the roof. "I remember playing on the swings and slide in the garden. And didn't we have a picnic under some huge tree?"

"The great oak." Aunty Connie

grinned. "Here, check this out." She pointed to a poster on the glass door.

Spellcroft Fair at The Oaks. Everyone welcome! International food stalls, plants, games, live bands and more. Celebrate our community and SAVE OUR CENTRE!

"Oh no – is The Oaks closing?" asked Jenny.

"Not if I can help it!" Aunty Connie replied. "The council are thinking of building a shopping complex in the area, which would probably mean demolishing the community centre.

I've organised this fair to showcase all the amazing classes and groups we run here, and I've invited some of the councillors to join us. I really hope we can prove that the centre is worth saving." Aunty Connie kissed her jade pendant for luck.

DRR DRRR DRRR DRRR DRRRRR.

Jenny jumped. A pneumatic drill drowned out all other sounds. A yellow sign on a fenced-off section of scrubland next to The Oaks read: "Warning! Construction Site". Workers in yellow hi-vis jackets were standing around the drill, piles of earth heaped up around the hole they had made.

"Have they started the building work already?" Jenny shouted over the noise.

"They're just doing some exploratory digging work first, apparently. But when our fair is the best ever, they'll have to reconsider." Aunty Connie raised her voice to be heard over the drilling. "Hey! Why don't you audition to perform at the fair? You're wicked on the drums!"

Jenny shook her head immediately. "Not on my own. No way."

Aunty Connie put an arm around her. "You're about to make loads of friends at your new school, remember? Maybe you'll start your own band!"

Jenny had wondered what it would feel like to be at a school long enough to make some proper friends for once. She looked around at the other kids

making their way to her school in their Spellcroft High blazers. There was a girl who looked about Jenny's age, walking with an older boy who looked like he might be her

brother. Both were tall with shiny black hair. Jenny's eye was drawn to the girl's hairclip, which twinkled in the sunlight. It was a beautiful gold leaf shape, with dangling gold chains threaded with tiny beads. The girl turned and noticed Jenny looking. Jenny dropped her gaze, feeling embarrassed.

Two girls crossed the street at the

zebra crossing. One had braids with purple beads, and her shorter friend had a mop of brown curls and rows of friendship bracelets on her wrists. The girls shared a smile as they walked, and they seemed to be deep in conversation.

Jenny suddenly felt very lonely.

DDDDDDDRRRRRRRRR . . .

The vibrations from the drilling shuddered up through her new school shoes as she walked.

CLANNNNGGGGG . . .
KERRRRUNNNCCCCCHHHH!!!

Jenny slammed her hands over her ears. A strange buzz rushed through her body. She looked down to see a line of light streaking across the ground. A fierce hissing noise erupted from the ground and a dazzling burst of light shot out of the drilling site. The workman operating the digger scrambled out of the cabin, looking shocked.

"Ewwww – what's that?" someone shouted as a cloud of green smoke curled up out of the hole in the ground.

"It stinks of rotten egg!" Aunty Connie said, pinching her nose with one hand.

Jenny's eyes watered.

The ground beneath Jenny's feet began to shake. Piles of earth around the hole had started crumbling away.

"It's a sinkhole – get back!" shouted the builder.

Jenny looked down to see that she was somehow teetering right at the edge of the growing hole!

Aunty Connie scrambled back, but Jenny slipped on the crumbling soil, her hands flailing out for balance. Aunty Connie tried to grab her, but it was no use – she missed Jenny by inches.

WHAM! Jenny fell flat on her back. Her wrist burned, but she hadn't injured it – it was her bracelet, glowing bright green, as if a fire had been lit inside the jade.

A tingling sensation filled Jenny's head, like when she drank lemonade too quickly and the bubbles went up her nose. But the pressure was more intense, growing stronger and stronger, until she felt her head might explode.

Jenny's heart banged hard and fast. *What's happening to me?* Vibrations ran up and down her body and then she felt herself go limp.

The pressure released . . . and suddenly Jenny was floating, drifting towards the clouds.

She felt light and no longer afraid. *That's funny* . . . She almost giggled as she watched the gaping sinkhole grow smaller below her. The green smoke that had been rising from the hole was now still, as were the people running away. Their arms and legs were suspended in running poses, as if someone had pressed pause on a remote.

The girl with the awesome braids clutched the front of her friend's blazer, eyes wide with fear. On one of her fingers, a ring glowed ruby red. Her curly-haired friend leaned backwards, away from the hole, at an improbable angle. At her collar, a necklace glowed silvery white. The tall girl with the shiny hair had raised a hand in warning

towards her brother. Her leaf-shaped
hairclip shone like a golden flame in her
hair.

There was Aunty Connie in her
tangerine maxi dress, her mouth open
mid-yell. Her arms reached towards
a girl in a Spellcroft High blazer, who
had fallen half in and half out of the
sinkhole. The girl had a long black bob,
just like Jenny's. She also carried Jenny's
rucksack on her back, and on her wrist
was Jenny's new bracelet, which was
glowing bright green.

Wait. That's me!

Fear struck Jenny. No wonder she felt
so light – she'd left her body behind!

Am I dead? she wondered.

Jenny felt another tug. This time downwards. She was falling out of the sky!

Down . . . down . . . down . . . Jenny fell, drawn towards the gaping sinkhole and into the depths of the earth.

CHAPTER TWO

Jenny was deep underground, feeling the same strange weightlessness she'd experienced in the air above the sinkhole moments before. Sunlight streamed in from a jagged circle of daylight far above, like the light from a cinema projector. It illuminated the thick green mist swirling around her.

The bad smell was worse down here.

As her eyes adjusted to the dim light, Jenny noticed strange symbols carved into the rock wall: mysterious swirls, spirals and arrows. They glittered like fiery sparklers on Bonfire Night. Below her, Jenny could see a crack in the ground out of which green mist was billowing, thick as fog on a winter's day.

The atmosphere felt damp and heavy. Jenny felt her energy draining away and she sank on to the cavern floor. She fell to her knees, head bowed.

Fight it. You must fight! a voice rang out in Jenny's head, like a bell. She jolted to her senses and felt a prickling sensation on the back of her neck.

Someone, or something, was watching her.

Jenny forced herself back up on to her feet and scanned the cavern carefully, grateful for the daylight shining down from the hole. She felt so, so heavy, like she could hardly move or cry for help. There was something evil down here – she could feel it.

Just then, a booming groan erupted from the crack in the ground. Something terrible, buried deep within the earth, was stirring to life.

"Who – who's there?" Jenny

whispered, her eyes wide with terror.

A dark gust of green mist curled out of the fissures and whirled around Jenny's ankles. Jenny forced herself to move. She scrambled backwards, pressing herself against the wall of the cave and kicking at the stinking fumes.

"I sense you have power within you. But it is not strong enough. You are not

strong enough to defeat me."

The voice that came from the green mist was dead and flat. Cold dread ran down Jenny's spine. The green vapour crept higher, wrapping around Jenny like vines.

"Get off me!" she cried, gasping for breath.

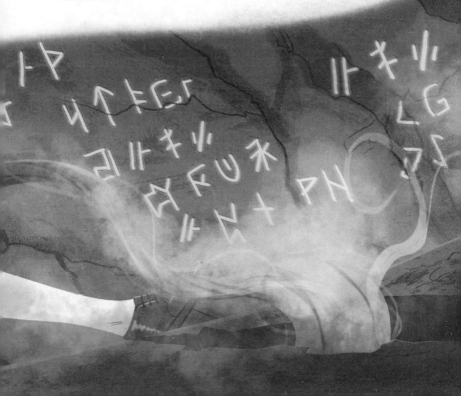

She touched her bracelet for comfort and it felt hot on her wrist.

The green vapour retreated with an angry hiss.

Jenny's bracelet glowed brighter still. It lit up the cave and gave Jenny courage. She felt her body moving upwards as her feet rose off the cavern floor.

"Who are you?" Jenny demanded as she began to float.

"Who am I?" sneered the voice. "I am your true nature. I am the voice in your head that hates and envies others. I am the part of you that you try to hide."

The green mist gathered once more,

circling Jenny as though taunting her. It whispered poisonous words into her ear. "Look around you. Nothing moves in this world but you and me. We are kindred spirits. Do not deny the hatred that lies in your heart. In ALL human hearts."

Fight back, a different voice said. This one was kind and encouraging.

"I'm nothing like you," Jenny stammered. "And I don't belong down here."

"Nor I. I belong in your world, and I shall return to it soon enough. Discord is my food, chaos is my drink. The more people fear me, the stronger I will become . . . strong enough to rule over you all."

Fear filled Jenny and a gust of wind tore around the cavern, engulfing her in dense, dark green fumes. Jenny began sinking to the floor again. *Noooo!*

The spirit cackled. "See how your fear has already strengthened me!"

"I don't fear you!" Jenny lied. She thought of her body lying helplessly next to the sinkhole.

"Soon you will. You all will. Poor, poor humans. So weak," the voice said coldly.

Jenny felt a surge of anger. *I am not weak!* She shut her eyes and gripped her jade bracelet, blocking out the spirit's whispers from her mind. She focused her energy on picturing herself rising, rising, back up to street level . . . Back to the kids in the Spellcroft High blazers and the builders in their hi-vis jackets. Back to Aunty Connie . . .

And then Jenny felt that tugging feeling again, except this time she was being pulled up.

Up, up and up . . .

She rushed towards the circle of daylight, until she was out of the sinkhole and floating in the sky. The spirit's voice called out to her from the cavern, growing fainter as she rose.

"Heed my warning. Now that I have been released from my prison, I am free to enter your world to begin my path of destruction. You are not strong enough to stop me on your own. Mayhem shall reign again!"

Jenny forced herself to focus not on the haunting voice, but on returning to her body. Willing herself ever upwards, she floated out of the sinkhole and shifted her concentration to the scene below. The schoolgirls she'd noticed earlier were still frozen in the same positions, and their jewellery was still glowing.

Jenny clutched her own glowing bracelet and stared down at her body, visualising herself moving her arms and legs. "Please help me," she whispered. She lurched forward, back into her body. Suddenly she found herself collapsed on the edge of the sinkhole, heart racing.

"Jenny," Aunty Connie cried, pulling her niece up into a fierce hug. "I thought I'd lost you!" Aunty Connie brushed dirt off Jenny's school uniform and helped her away from the sinkhole. "I'm calling the council. There's no way they should be building anything here; it's way too dangerous!"

"What do you think—"

"Oh no, and now you're going to be late! I promised your mum I'd look after you and you've nearly been eaten by a sinkhole before we've even got to school. Thank goodness we're wearing our good luck charms!"

Jenny glanced at her bracelet. It had lost its glow and felt cool once more. *You don't know the half of it, Aunty Connie . . .*

CHAPTER THREE

The final morning bell was ringing as Jenny waved goodbye to Aunty Connie and hurried into school.

Jenny caught a glimpse of the three girls from the building site up ahead. She wanted to call after them, but the woman on the reception desk insisted on walking with her to her new Year

Seven form room. She waved Jenny inside and the classroom teacher clapped her hands for silence. "Good morning, Jenny. I'm Miss Rabette. Welcome to 7R. Everyone, let's say hello to Jenny Lee. It's her first day at Spellcroft High."

"Good morning, Jenny," chorused the class, sounding bored.

Miss Rabette tucked a lock of salt-and-pepper hair behind her ear and addressed the class. "I want you all to make Jenny feel welcome." The teacher smiled at Jenny and gestured for her to take the only empty seat. "Ananya, perhaps you would like to show Jenny to her first lesson?"

The girl gave Jenny a swift smile
and then put her head down to write
something in her notebook. *The tall girl
from the building site!* Jenny glanced at
her hairclip, but there was no glow.

When the bell rang for the first lesson,
Ananya looked over Jenny's shoulder at
her timetable. "You've got English first
– follow me."

Ananya strode off with Jenny trailing
behind. Jenny would have liked to ask
Ananya about what had happened at
the sinkhole, but the corridors were too
busy to have a proper conversation.
Jenny still couldn't get the spirit's cold,

dead voice out of her head: *You are not strong enough to stop me on your own.*

The rest of the morning's lessons went by in a whirl, and it was all Jenny could do to keep up and not get totally lost.

Finally, the bell rang for lunch and Jenny followed the crowds to the canteen. She scanned the room looking for Ananya, but she couldn't spot her. Jenny sat down surrounded by groups of chattering friends and took her lunchbox out of her rucksack. A garlicky smell wafted out when she opened the lid. Gong Gong's noodles with meatballs was one of Jenny's favourite dishes, but she had lost her appetite. She hated eating alone.

The last lesson of the day was music, and Jenny had to admit that the music hall was impressive. There was a stage at the front and a grand piano in the corner. Instead of desks, there were plastic chairs with tables on the arms. The two other girls from the building site were sitting next to each other, and Jenny's heart beat fast as she quickly made her way over to sit next to them before she lost her nerve.

The music teacher, Mr Pereira, called for attention and ran his hand through his mop of hair. "Can you get into groups of four, please?"

Jenny cleared her throat nervously, turning to the two friends. "Hi, can I join your group? I'm Jenny. I think I saw you both this morning before school – at the building site?"

The girl with the braids turned to Jenny and smiled. Jenny noticed she had freckles sprinkled over her nose. "Of course – I knew you looked familiar! I'm Tamzin, and this is Maya."

"Hey, Jenny! Nice bracelet." Maya grinned, revealing a gap between her front teeth.

"We just need one more – hey!" Jenny

waved at Ananya, who was sitting alone. "Do you want to join us?"

"Sure," Ananya said, picking up her bag and walking over.

"It's Ananya, right?" Tamzin said.

Ananya nodded.

"You were there this morning too," said Maya. "How are you finding Spellcroft High so far?"

"It's OK," said Ananya with a shrug. "I'm the only one from my primary school who came here, so I'm still kind of getting used to it."

Jenny felt a little less alone, hearing that Ananya didn't know many people at Spellcroft High either.

Mr Pereira clapped his hands for quiet. "Right, Jenny, let's get you up to speed. We've been practising an old folk tune called the 'The Great Oak Tree'. The Celts named the oak tree the King of the Trees because they believed oak trees could channel magical properties. In fact, this particular folk song is thought to originate from Spellcroft itself."

Mr Pereira walked over to the piano. "Tamzin, could you sing it for us, please?"

Tamzin stood up, looking nervous.

"Go on, Tamzin, you can do it!" Maya squeezed her hand.

The teacher played a medieval-sounding intro, and Tamzin took a deep breath and sang. Her voice rang out across the music hall. It was beautiful.

"Come with me to the great oak tree,
Come and sing and dance with me.
Together we are stronger by the great oak tree.
Together we stand, brave, bold and free."

"Wow, Tamzin! You're such a good singer," whispered Jenny as Tamzin sat down to applause.

"Thanks!" Tamzin replied, smiling.

Mr Pereira clapped for attention. "Now, in your groups, please find a practice room and come up with your own interpretation of the song." He handed out copies of the music to the students filing out of the music hall. "You could sing in rounds. Or, if someone plays an instrument, they can accompany the singers."

"This one's free," said Tamzin, opening the door to an empty practice room. Jenny gasped as she stepped inside – there was a drum kit!

"I'll take the drums, if no one minds?" she said.

"Sure! I play the cello, but I think I'll stick to vocals," said Tamzin.

"I'll do backing vocals," Ananya said.

"And I'll play the guitar," said Maya, picking one up and slinging the strap confidently across her body.

Jenny sat at the drums and sped through her favourite beats, which

earned an approving nod from Ananya.

"Hey, look at this," Tamzin said, showing the others the sheet music. "Mr Pereira's added a few facts about the song. '*Druids used to conduct ceremonies in oak woods, to call upon their protection against evil spirits.*'"

Evil spirits. Jenny's heart pounded in her chest. She had to ask them. *It's now or never.* She suppressed a shiver and put her drumsticks down. "Do you think there really are such things as evil spirits?"

The others blinked at Jenny.

"Or – or magic?" Jenny said quickly. "Like, at the building site this morning.

Did anyone else feel something . . . magical happen?"

Ananya shifted in her seat and Tamzin slowly put down the sheet music.

"What do you mean?" Maya asked, her eyes wide.

Jenny continued, words tumbling out of her mouth. "Something really weird happened. I – I think I had some sort of out-of-body experience when that sinkhole opened. I fell, then my bracelet started glowing . . . and then, all of a sudden, I was floating out of my body. I was pulled down into the sinkhole, into an evil spirit's lair. I think my bracelet's magic saved me from it."

Maya, Ananya and Tamzin were stunned into silence, looking at Jenny with their mouths open.

Oh no, they don't believe me, thought Jenny. *This is turning out to be the worst first day ever!*

Ananya was the first to speak. "Maybe you banged your head when you fell?"

"You mean you guys didn't feel anything?" Jenny looked around desperately. "Your hairclip was glowing, Ananya, and so were Tamzin's ring and Maya's necklace."

Tamzin nodded slowly. "I don't know if it was magic, but something weird did happen to my ring! And to Maya's necklace. We've been talking about it all day, haven't we, Maya?"

"Yeah," Maya breathed. "Do you think it *was* magic? Like, for real?!"

Jenny's insides melted with relief. "Yes, I do, actually."

Tamzin held her hand close to her face. She stared hard at her ring, but it didn't glow or heat up. "It would be so awesome if my ring was magic."

"Shall we try saying a spell or something?" Maya suggested.

"What, like proper witches and wizards?" Ananya asked.

Tamzin laughed. "I'll give it a go and

55

see what happens." She touched her ring and sat up straight. "Abracadabra! Shala – shalakazam? Erm . . . bippity-boppity-boo!"

Is that sunlight catching Tamzin's ring? No, her ring was definitely sparkling on its own. It glowed a faint red colour, and a gust of wind blew through the practice room, rattling the windows. When Jenny looked again, Tamzin's ring had already dimmed.

"Did you see that?" asked Jenny.

"See what?" Ananya asked.

"Your ring glowed! It *is* magic!" said Maya.

"I felt a tingling in my fingertips,

like something was there, desperate to burst out. I think I summoned that gust of wind! Maya, you have a go!" said Tamzin, eyes shining with excitement.

Maya touched her necklace, her brow furrowed in concentration, and said, "Hocus pocus, let's focus!" For a brief moment, Maya's necklace shimmered with an iridescent white light.

"My hand's tingling!" Maya exclaimed with a smile.

Jenny was sure she saw two pointy teeth poking out of Maya's mouth. *Wait! Were those . . . fangs?!*

Then, just as quickly as Tamzin's ring had done, Maya's necklace dimmed and the fangs vanished.

Ananya shook her head. "I just don't see it, guys. The sinkhole this morning was caused by the drilling. The bad smell was probably caused by a gas leak, which is why everyone felt funny. Magic can't be real."

"But I saw your hairclip glowing too," insisted Jenny.

Ananya put her hand up to her hair and touched the gold clip. "It's really shiny, Jenny. It glints in the sun."

Suddenly, Jenny's drumsticks flew up in the air and landed on the ground with a clatter.

Jenny gasped. She hadn't touched them. They had definitely moved on their own.

Ananya looked startled and let go of her hairclip. Before Jenny could ask her if she'd made the drumsticks move, there was a knock on the door. Mr Pereira popped his head into the room. "We're meeting back in the hall in fifteen minutes so each group can share what they've done."

"Maybe we should practise the song," said Tamzin when Mr Pereira had left. "I don't want to get into trouble."

"Sure," said Jenny, picking up her drumsticks. And as she beat out the rhythm, her mind was racing with what she had just discovered.

They felt the magic too – even Ananya. It wasn't just me!

"Good work, guys. Keep practising in your groups this week," Mr Pereira said as the class streamed out of his lesson.

"Hey, I loved your drum riffs, Jenny," said Maya as they packed their bags.

"Yeah, you were awesome," added Tamzin. "So were you, Ananya. We sounded great together."

Jenny remembered what Aunty Connie had told her that morning. She decided to take a risk. "Maybe we should form a band? My Aunty Connie runs The Oaks, and they're holding auditions to perform at the Spellcroft Fair next week. What do you think?"

"I'm up for performing," said Maya.

"I'm in!" said Tamzin. "Sounds fun."

"What about you, Ananya?" asked Jenny. "We could use your harmonies."

"I don't know . . . I don't play an instrument, and Tamzin's an amazing singer on her own. You don't really need me." Ananya waved goodbye and headed off to find her brother.

Ananya knows more than she's letting on – I can feel it, thought Jenny.

"I reckon she'll come around," said Tamzin confidently. "Who wouldn't want to be in a band?"

"Maybe the magic stuff is freaking her out?" said Maya, linking arms with Jenny as the three girls set off for home.

"We live in a place called Spellcroft, after all," said Tamzin. "It makes total sense that we can do magic!"

Jenny said goodbye to Maya and Tamzin at the corner of her road, and walked the rest of the way home in high spirits. She was glad she hadn't had the chance to tell her new friends the whole story about the evil spirit. That would have really freaked Ananya out. Jenny didn't want to scare them – that was exactly what the spirit wanted.

She shivered, hearing the spirit's croaky voice ringing in her head once more: *The more people fear me, the stronger I will become.*

CHAPTER FOUR

Jenny lifted her face towards the September sunshine, which poured down like liquid gold over Spellcroft Street.

"Are you looking forward to seeing your new friends?" asked Por Por as they walked past the park, its duck pond sparkling in the autumnal light.

"Can't wait," Jenny replied.

Jenny was meeting Maya and Tamzin at the Bubble Tea Café to discuss their new band and hopefully practise spells! They'd invited Ananya too, but she'd said she was busy. Jenny felt a bit nervous about meeting Maya and Tamzin outside of school. Jenny wasn't even sure she had magic powers after all. Would they still want to be in a band with her?

She had tried to make her bracelet glow loads of times over the last week – rubbing it, saying any magic words she could think of, but nothing had worked. *Or maybe my powers only work when I'm in serious trouble, facing down an evil spirit?* Jenny shivered despite the warmth of the day.

"Hello, Mrs Chen!" Por Por greeted the owner of the Bubble Tea Café in Mandarin as they walked in. Mrs Chen was a striking woman with leopard-print glasses and blue streaks in her black hair. "No other customers today?"

The shelves behind the counter were lined with glass jars of round boba and cubes of jelly. The café was colourful, with turquoise walls and empty cherry-red seats.

"Too sunny. Everyone's at the park,

I think." Mrs Chen shrugged, tying a watermelon-print apron round her waist. "What can I get you?"

"I'll have a mango milk tea with strawberry popping boba and tapioca pearls, please," Jenny said. She spotted Tamzin and Maya tucked in a corner booth. "My friends are here," she told Por Por, waving at them.

"Go sit, I'll bring it over." Mrs Chen smiled and scooped up boba from one of the jars, her brass bangles jangling.

Por Por kissed Jenny goodbye. "Make sure you walk home together, *bao-beh*. I'll see you later."

Jenny walked over to the corner

booth, where Tamzin and Maya were discussing something animatedly.

"Wait till you hear this!" said Maya as Jenny joined them. Maya looked as though she was about to explode while they waited for Jenny's drink. When Mrs Chen had come and gone, Maya propped the menus up around their table so they had some privacy.

"Tell her, Tamzin," squeaked Maya.

"I'd been doing some research online when I came across this old website that explained how to channel your magic powers. For example, if you draw your magic from an object such as a wand or a talisman – like my ring—" Tamzin waggled her ring finger at Jenny, "—then you need to touch your object and say a rhyming spell. Here, listen to this." Tamzin closed her eyes and touched her ring.

"*Precious ring, ruby glow,*
Come and let my magic flow!"

Tamzin's ring glowed red, and as she lifted her hands, a gust of wind swirled around the booth, knocking over the menus. Tamzin twirled her finger around and a mini whirlwind danced on the table in front of Maya and Jenny, making them gasp.

"Wow!" said Jenny in amazement.

Tamzin fell back in her seat, letting go of her ring. The wind immediately disappeared. She took a long, shaky breath. "That. Was. Intense!"

"How did you know the words to say?" Jenny asked.

Tamzin slid a notebook out of her bag. She opened it to pages full of crossed-out spells and highlighted words. "You've got to call the magic to your object. I had lots of false starts, but once I tried this spell, my ring glowed hot and my fingertips tingled. I imagined what I wanted to happen and – *boom* – it worked!"

"Amazing," breathed Maya.

Tamzin grinned proudly. Jenny gave her a high five.

"I've managed to use my magic, but I still don't think this is the right spell for my ring," said Tamzin. "The wind I'm calling is really weak, and it doesn't last very long."

"I've been doing a little detective work too," said Maya, patting her necklace. "This was handed down to me from my grandma, Bebe – and she got it from *her* grandma, so who knows how long it's been in my family? And you know my grandmother was from Egypt, right? Well, this necklace could be really old – look!" Maya took off the chain and showed Jenny and Tamzin the back of the pendant, tracing a fingertip over a faint engraving on the silver. "See this word? *Sehr*. Bebe said it means magic in Arabic."

"Cool!" said Jenny. "My bracelet's been passed down in my family for generations too."

"So has my ring!" Tamzin exclaimed. "Maybe that's important. Hey, what's that on the other side of your pendant, Maya?"

Maya flipped over the pendant so they could see another engraving, which depicted an ancient Egyptian woman with a cat's head.

Jenny remembered the fangs she'd seen at school when Maya smiled. "Maybe you've got the power to shapeshift into a cat!"

"How cool would that be?" said Maya. "Let me try making up a spell." Maya held her necklace tight and scrunched up her eyes and nose in concentration.

"Silver necklace from the past,
Give me magic in a blast!"

Maya's necklace glowed silvery white and her ears became long and pointed,

with fine, silky fur
shooting upwards
at the tips. Maya
twitched her
nose and let
out a croaky,
unpractised meow.

Jenny and
Tamzin stared,
wide-eyed. Then
Maya opened her eyes and let go of
her necklace. The magical connection
was lost in an instant and Maya's ears
shrank back to normal.

"You started turning into a cat!"
gasped Tamzin. "How did you do it?"

"I said the spell, and I felt warm inside, like magic from the necklace was pouring through me," Maya said, her eyes sparkling. "Then I imagined I was a cat. I pictured myself licking my paws and I could feel myself changing shape!"

"You try, Jenny!" said Tamzin.

"Erm, let me see . . ." Jenny muttered nervously. She touched her bracelet and concentrated hard. She tried to think of a spell like the ones her friends had said.

"Lucky bracelet made of jade,
Please send magic to my aid!"

Nothing happened. Jenny opened her eyes a peep and glanced down at her bracelet. It wasn't glowing at all.

She looked over at Maya and Tamzin and shrugged.

"Don't worry, Jenny – it will come," said Tamzin kindly.

What if it doesn't, though?

Jenny shivered, thinking again of the evil spirit. It had said she wasn't powerful enough to stop it on her own. What if she wasn't powerful at all?

The bell above the door tinkled, interrupting Jenny's thoughts.

"It's Ananya!" Maya whispered. "She said she was busy."

"Maybe she's changed her mind about the band," said Maya.

Ananya walked over to the counter. "One peach tea, please, with kiwi popping boba and raspberry jelly."

Mrs Chen scooped boba and jelly into a tall glass and added peach tea. "I need to get more straws. One minute." She disappeared into the kitchen. Ananya waited with her back to the others.

As usual, Ananya's hair was held back on one side by the leaf-shaped clip. She reached her hand up and touched it.

Jenny watched, astonished, as the hairclip began to glow. She gasped as bright pink boba levitated out of a jar on the counter and hovered in the air!

Jenny nudged Tamzin and Maya as more strawberry boba floated out of the jar and then drifted towards the glass of peach tea. Maya leaned forward to get a closer look, accidentally knocking a menu over.

Ananya turned sharply at the sound and let go of her hairclip. The boba fell, splashing into her drink.

"Here we are!" Mrs Chen came back with a pack of straws and handed one to Ananya. "I'll be doing inventory out back – if you need anything, just ring the bell on the counter."

"Ananya!" called Tamzin, waving.

Jenny scooted along the bench to make room for Ananya. "We saw you do magic, Ananya – you can't deny it!"

Ananya grinned. "OK, I admit it!" She leaned forward and lowered her voice. "I've been practising at home, but this is the best it has worked so far."

"What did you do?" asked Maya.

"I touched my hairclip and wished really hard for the boba to move, and it did!" said Ananya.

"And you moved my drumsticks, at music practice," Jenny said.

"I have no idea how I did that, Jenny, honest," said Ananya earnestly. "I was just wishing for you to stop asking me questions. I was so freaked out by what happened at the building site. When the sinkhole opened up, my lunch bag almost fell in, but I somehow made it come back to me."

"Why didn't you tell us this before?" asked Maya.

"I am really sorry I didn't." Ananya cast her eyes down and shrugged. "I've been trying so hard to blend in at Spellcroft High and not be different; getting magic powers was the last thing I needed. I just don't want anyone to think I'm weird."

"I get it, starting a new school is

hard," said Jenny, putting an arm around Ananya. "But you're not alone any more. Us four, we're all magic. We *are* different."

Maya and Tamzin nodded.

Ananya smiled and took a sip of her drink. "Thanks, Jenny. I suppose magic is pretty cool! Although mine only works some of the time."

"We're starting to figure out how it works." Tamzin showed Ananya her notebook. "I had to say a rhyming spell."

"And I pictured what I wanted to happen," added Maya.

"Your hairclip was glowing when you

were at the counter," said Jenny. "Has it been in your family a long time? We think we each have a magical object." She held up her wrist. "Mine's my jade bracelet."

Ananya's eyes widened. "Yes! My hairclip's really old. It used to belong to my great-aunt, who lives in India."

Tamzin checked her watch. "Listen – we should probably talk about the audition."

"Um, about that – can I join your band too, if I'm not too late?" asked Ananya shyly.

"You're not too late!" Tamzin smiled. "I even wrote a harmony for you. I was hoping you'd change your mind."

Ananya smiled with relief.

Tamzin showed Ananya the harmony. Jenny drummed a beat on the table and they all began to sing together. "*Come with me . . .*"

"*To the great oak tree . . .*" Ananya added a lower harmony, and then Jenny and Maya joined in with the chorus.

Suddenly Maya stopped singing and pinched her nose. "Eww, what's that smell?"

A stinky rotten-egg smell hit Jenny's nostrils. It reminded her of the sinkhole in the street . . .

Tamzin looked down at her tea and

screamed. The boba in her glass had transformed from pink to slimy green. There were dark dots in the middle of each jellied sphere. *Just like frogspawn.*

"Uggggh, your drink!" Maya cried.

It wasn't just Tamzin's drink – all the boba had turned into green, slimy frogspawn!

The stench spread through the café and a green mist drifted under the door, curling around the girls' feet. They leapt up on to their seats and Jenny watched in horror as the black dots in the slimy frogspawn grew, changing shape and turning into tadpoles. The tadpoles wriggled, pushing their way out of the jelly balls, and started darting around the tea.

"This can't be happening," Jenny muttered. But the tadpoles had already sprouted little legs with tiny webbed feet. In seconds, hundreds of small, green, slimy frogs were jumping out of their glasses. They hopped on to the table and swarmed across the floor.

Maya screwed her eyes shut. "I hate frogs!"

The creatures hopped on to the counter and into the boba jars. Boba and jelly shot out of them and splattered all over the café, making a big sticky mess.

"AARGH!" Maya screeched as a slimy frog hopped up on to her shoulder and then into her hair.

"We need to do something!" shouted Tamzin.

Maya's eyes were still squeezed shut, but Jenny noticed her necklace was shining with magical light.

"Maya, your necklace. It's glowing!" cried Jenny as a cold, slimy frog hopped on to her foot and croaked at her. "Try doing some magic."

"Urrgggh – frogs! I can't bear it . . ."
Maya said, cringing in fright.

"Be brave!" Jenny urged. "You're not
alone."

"Try using the word on your necklace,
Maya," said Tamzin, brushing a frog
off her head.

Maya held on tightly to her pendant
and, as if in a trance, she chanted a
spell:

"Sehr *swirling like a wave,*
Ancient powers, make me brave."

The necklace glowed brighter and
brighter, suddenly flashing as bright as a

star. Jenny watched as Maya shimmered and then – *POOF!* – disappeared.

Jenny, Ananya and Tamzin stared at each other in disbelief as frogs continued to hop wildly around the café.

"What just happened?" asked Jenny.

"Where's Maya?" Tamzin said, sounding worried.

"Woof!" They looked down. A cute little puppy with curly black fur was sitting where Maya had been a moment before. Jenny stared in disbelief. The puppy was wearing Maya's silver necklace around its neck like a collar.

"Maya?" whispered Tamzin, kneeling

down. "Is that you?"

The puppy woofed again and wagged its tail. It gave another bark, then chased after the hopping frogs. The little dog rounded the frogs up and herded them into a corner of the café.

"Go, Maya!" said Ananya, opening

the door of the café.

The girls watched through the café window as the puppy drove the frogs outside. She herded them to the park across the street and into a pond. Maya yapped and bounded back to the café, wagging her tail proudly.

"What's going on here?" Mrs Chen came back into the shop, skidding to a stop when she saw the mess. The green mist had dispersed, but the floor was strewn with spilt drinks, knocked-over chairs and boba. Her cheeks grew pink with anger. She pointed at the puppy with a shaking finger. "Did you sneak a dog in here?"

"No, but—" Jenny began.

"Get it out of here, right this second!" Mrs Chen cried. "No pets allowed!" She grabbed a brush and began angrily sweeping the floor.

"We're really sorry," said Jenny. The girls hurried outside with Maya close on their heels. Jenny hoped Mrs Chen wouldn't tell Por Por what had happened. She'd be grounded for a year and a half!

"This way," said Tamzin, leading them down an alleyway. When they were sure they were alone, Tamzin crouched next to the puppy. "Maya? You can change back now."

For a moment, nothing happened.
The girls exchanged worried glances.

"How's she going to say her spell?
Dogs can't talk . . ." Ananya whispered.

Jenny held her breath, waiting
anxiously.

The puppy pawed at the necklace
around its neck, which started glowing.

"Come on, Maya, you can do it,"
Jenny whispered.

There was a sudden shimmer of white
magic from Maya's necklace, and Jenny
watched in amazement as the puppy's
front paws turned into hands and
its stubby back legs lengthened. The
puppy shook its head and its curly fur

transformed into Maya's mop of brown curls. Moments later, Maya's head morphed back into her face. Back to her human self again, Maya crouched on the pavement, breathing hard.

Tamzin helped her stand up. "Oh, Maya!" she cried, hugging her friend. "Are you OK?"

"I'm fine," Maya said shakily.

"How did it feel?" Jenny asked.

"Weird," said Maya, catching her breath. "Weird, but awesome too! I felt my necklace get warm, and when Tamzin reminded me about the word on my talisman, the right spell just came to me."

"It was like you knew what to say," said Ananya.

Maya nodded. "That was *sehr*. It felt like it wasn't me saying the spell, but something speaking through me, if that makes any sense. Someone familiar, but not . . ." Maya seemed lost for words for a moment. "I pictured myself turning into a massive, scary dog to chase the frogs away. Is that what happened?"

"Well, you were more of a puppy," said Jenny. "But it worked. You got rid of the frogs."

"It was so magical, Maya. You can shapeshift!" Tamzin said in awe.

Ananya frowned. "But where did those frogs come from? And that green mist and the bad smell?"

"It stank like when the builders opened up the sinkhole last week," said Maya.

Jenny's tummy flipped with nerves. It was time to trust her friends and tell them everything. "Remember when I said I was pulled into an evil spirit's lair at the sinkhole?"

The others nodded.

Jenny took a deep breath. "Well . . . when I was down there, the evil spirit told me that it was going to return to our world and create chaos. It said the more people fear it, the stronger it becomes. I think the evil spirit did this, to scare us." Jenny looked down and let her hair fall over her face. "I'm sorry – I should have told you the whole story in music class."

"I didn't really give you a chance, to be fair," said Ananya, reaching over to put her arm around Jenny. Tamzin and Maya joined in on the other side.

"I was scared you wouldn't believe me if I told you everything," admitted Jenny.

"Of course we believe you," Tamzin said. "And we're going to stop this evil spirit together."

CHAPTER FIVE

The next day, Aunty Connie found the girls a spare room at The Oaks so they could rehearse for their audition. Jenny set up the drum kit and Maya tuned her electric guitar.

"*Come with me to the great oak tree,*" Tamzin's voice rang out. Ananya harmonised as Maya strummed a chord and Jenny added the beats.

They were just getting into their new arrangement when the door opened and Aunty Connie burst in, looking dismayed.

"What's the matter?" asked Jenny.

"Vandals! They've sprayed graffiti all over the wall outside. The paint's fresh, so it must have only just happened."

The girls followed Aunty Connie outside and round to the back of The Oaks. The sinkhole across the street seemed wider than before, and crowds of protesters had gathered nearby. Some wanted to stop the building work, while others wanted it to go ahead. They all seemed angry, regardless of what side they were on, and shouted slogans at each other.

The back wall of the community centre had been sprayed with bright green graffiti. With a sinking feeling, Jenny recognised the strange symbols that had glittered on the cavern walls. There was also a message: *Nothing will stop me!* Underneath the message was a scrawled tag signature. *The Graydig.*

"This has to be the work of someone who wants the construction to go ahead." Aunty Connie raked a hand through her hair. "It's the last thing I need. I'm worried The Oaks won't look like the sort of place people will want to save with all this horrible graffiti."

"We can clean it for you!" said Jenny.

"I've got a better idea," said Ananya. "We can paint over it!"

"We can make a mural!" said Maya.

"Are you sure?" Aunty Connie asked. The girls nodded and Aunty Connie sighed with relief. "That would be a massive help. Thank you, girls. I'm so busy organising the fair. There's loads of paint in the art room."

"I don't think protesters did this," said Jenny as the girls walked back outside holding paints and brushes. "I saw symbols like the graffiti ones at the bottom of the sinkhole, where I heard the voice." Jenny touched the writing with her finger. "*The Graydig*. Could this be the spirit's name?"

"If the Graydig, or whatever it's called, really did create this mess, then we're going to make the wall look ten times better!" Tamzin said confidently.

"What should we paint?" asked Ananya.

"How about a big oak tree to offer protection against evil spirits?" asked Maya.

"Yeah," said Jenny, steadying herself. If it was good enough for the druids hundreds of years ago, maybe it would be good enough for the girls now.

Jenny and her friends sang again as they started to paint.

"*Come with me to the great oak tree,*" Tamzin sang as she brushed paint up and down.

"*Come and sing and dance with me,*" Ananya added in harmony, and Jenny and Maya tapped some beats with their paintbrushes.

Soon, the graffiti was covered by an oak tree, with a knobbly trunk and green-leafed branches heavy with acorns. But soon, over the smell of the paint, Jenny could smell something else. Something foul.

"Oh no . . . not again!" Maya dropped her brush and covered her nose with her hand.

"It stinks!" said Tamzin, scowling.

From the sinkhole came a howl of sinister laughter. Goosebumps crept over Jenny's bare arms. Wisps of green smoke drifted over from the sinkhole.

"Uh-oh," said Ananya.

"I think you're right about the evil spirit, Jenny," said Tamzin.

The green mist thickened, enveloping the girls inside a thick fog.

Perhaps I can use my magic to help? thought Jenny. But worries about the evil spirit crowded into her mind and she couldn't focus. The bracelet remained cool against her wrist.

A dead, flat voice whispered on the breeze. *You have no control over your powers.* Jenny spun around, but there was nobody there.

Tamzin closed her eyes and touched her ring.

"*Precious ring, ruby glow,*
Come and let my magic flow . . ."

The ring glowed a faint ruby colour, and a faint breeze swirled round Tamzin. "My magic isn't strong enough," she said, frustrated.

"The wind still cleared the mist though, Tamzin!" replied Ananya. She was right. The mist was retreating with a hiss, back towards the sinkhole.

"Yes, but look!" said Tamzin, pointing up.

Jenny looked at their mural, her heart

sinking. More graffiti had appeared on the wall, this time out of the girls' reach, near the top.

In dark, menacing letters, it read: *The Graydig is back*.

Maya stood by Jenny, looking up at the graffiti. "Let me try. I know how my spells work now." She closed her eyes, touched her talisman and said a spell.

"Sehr *somewhere in the sky,*
Ancient powers, let me fly."

The other girls stared in amazement as Maya transformed into an emerald-coloured parakeet. She tried to pick up a paintbrush, but it was too heavy and slipped from her beak, clattering to the pavement. The parakeet squawked with frustration, flapping her wings.

Ananya stepped forward. She touched her talisman and whispered a wish under her breath.

Ananya's hairclip flashed gold. She fixed her concentration on her paintbrush. It trembled for a few moments, then flew straight into the air. It dipped itself in a pot of red paint and then hovered in front of the wall. With one long swish, it painted the first arch of a rainbow, starting to cover up the graffiti. Ananya let out a long breath and the paintbrush fell to the ground.

"I couldn't keep it going any longer," said Ananya, out of breath from the effort. "I wish I had more control over my powers."

"I'll get a ladder," said Jenny.

A few minutes later, Jenny propped a ladder against the wall and Ananya climbed up to finish painting the rainbow over the oak tree.

Maya the parakeet picked up a lighter paintbrush and fluttered up to add artistic swirls and loops to the mural.

The girls – and parakeet – worked hard. Soon, the painting of the large oak tree was beautifully framed by

bright flowers around
the base and a sparkling
rainbow over the top.
"Awesome!" said
Jenny, standing back to admire their
hard work. She was proud of what
they'd done and tried her best to push
away the thought that she was the only
one who hadn't been able to conjure up

any magic to help.

"I'm scared of the chaos the Graydig is going to cause next," Maya said, shaking the last feathers from her hair as she transformed back into a girl.

"That's what it wants," said Jenny. "To scare us."

"We beat it in the Bubble Tea Café, and we've beaten it again here," said Ananya, her eyes sparkling with defiance. "Our magic is getting stronger every day. We can find a way to defeat it; I just know we can."

Tamzin nodded, her eyes glittering. "The next time the Graydig strikes, we're going to be ready."

CHAPTER SIX

The next day, Jenny, Maya and Ananya were in the main hall at The Oaks, watching the auditions for the Spellcroft Fair and nervously waiting their turn. A street dance group finished an impressive routine. There was a burst of applause as the dancers took a bow and left the stage.

"Where's Tamzin?" Jenny said as the next audition group tested mics and plugged in electric guitars.

"I don't know," said Maya, her eyes flicking nervously to the clock on the wall.

The doors opened and Jenny looked round hopefully, but it was Aunty Connie backing into the room with a huge crate of houseplants and flowers for the plant stall at the fair. She set them on the floor at the back of the hall, where there were already several other plants that had been donated.

"Do you think Tamzin got the time wrong?" Ananya asked.

"She's never late," said Maya, biting her lip.

The band on stage finished their song to more applause.

"Jenny?" the director called. "Your band is up next."

"Stall for time," whispered Ananya.

Jenny took her time setting the drum kit up on the stage. *Where's Tamzin?* she wondered.

Maya spent ages looking around for an extension cord to plug in her amp.

"You really do need to start soon or you're going to lose your slot," said the director impatiently.

"Sorry I'm late!" Tamzin ran through

the doors and rushed on to the stage, looking flustered.

"We were worried something had happened to you," said Maya. "What's going on?"

"I'll explain later!" Tamzin said.

Jenny tapped her drumsticks together, counting them in. "One, two, three and four . . ."

"*Come with me to the great oak tree*," sang Tamzin and Ananya as the others played.

BANG!

The noise came from the bathroom at the back of the hall.

"Oh, what now!" said the director,

looking up. "And what's that disgusting smell?"

Putrid green water began flooding out from under the door of the bathroom. It stank like a sewer. It stank like the Graydig.

The other musicians, who'd been packing up their instruments, rushed out of the exit. Jenny heard Aunty Connie shouting from the corridor outside. "Everybody out! There must be a leaking pipe in the bathroom. I'm going to turn the water off at the mains."

Soon, Jenny, Ananya, Maya and Tamzin were the only ones left in the hall. There was a loud creak and the door to the bathroom burst open, a wave of filthy green water gushing out of it.

The power of the water was immense and in seconds the floor was completely submerged. Jenny stared, aghast, as the water crashed over the crates of houseplants and potted flowers, which wilted and shrivelled before her eyes.

"Quick, unplug the equipment before the water reaches the sockets," Tamzin warned as the water splashed up on to the stage.

"Oh no!" Maya cried. "My guitar will be ruined!"

The water was flooding in so fast it looked like the stage would soon be completely underwater.

"Leave it to me," said Tamzin. She touched her ring and focused. The ring glowed ruby red. Tamzin closed her eyes and became very still for a moment, breathing calmly. Then she chanted a spell:

"Idan, *strong as the winds that blow,*
Ancient powers, make the water go."

A fierce wind began to blow around the hall, whipping Tamzin's braids around her face. Her jacket billowed out behind

her like a sail. Bright, sparkling red
light shone out from Tamzin's ring and
engulfed her.

She stepped to the front of the stage
and repeated the spell, stretching out
her hand over the putrid water. The

wind whisked round
her, faster and
faster, like a
tornado with
Tamzin at its
centre.
Jenny,
Ananya
and Maya
looked on in

amazement. The wind obeyed Tamzin's every command. She moved her hands, directing the wind as it tore across the surface of the water. It picked up the scudding ripples, turning them into one gigantic wave. The funnel of frothing green water grew taller and taller until it was nearly at the ceiling, spinning around and spraying the girls with an icy cold mist. Faster and faster the whirlpool swirled, drawing all the water into its fierce orbit until it formed a giant column.

"Hold on, Tamzin," urged Jenny.

The magic her friend was using was the strongest Jenny had seen yet, and

Tamzin stumbled slightly under the pressure.

Whsssssshzzzzz whsssssshzzzzzz whsssssssshzzzzzzz . . .

Around the hall, posters were ripped from noticeboards, pulled by the centrifugal force of Tamzin's magic.

Tamzin's hands were shaking as she commanded the whirlpool across the hall, towards the window. It crashed open, smacking against the wall outside. The pane cracked.

Tamzin raised her arms into the air.

Jenny could feel the force of the wind now, lifting her up off the ground. "Aargh!" she cried.

Just when Jenny thought she would be blown away too, Tamzin cast the whirlpool through the window and out into the garden.

The trees outside bent in the wind, as if they were about to be ripped out by their roots. Rustling leaves and the sound of whizzing filled the air.

Jenny, Ananya and Maya ran to the window, watching in amazement. The giant whirlpool spun into the air, rising higher and higher until it disappeared into the clouds.

Tamzin fell to her knees, exhausted.

"You did it, Tamzin," cried Maya.

Tamzin hadn't finished though.

Seeming to move in a trance, she got back to her feet and walked towards the wilted plants and flowers at the back of the hall.

"Idan, *show me what you know,*
Ancient powers, make these plants
grow."

Shrivelled brown leaves opened out, growing healthy and green again. The wilted stems stood up, proud and tall once more. Flowers lifted their heads and drooping petals unfurled. Their colours shone, brighter than before: candy pink, vibrant orange,

deep red. Leaves turned lush emerald or bright jade. As the flowers and plants recovered, fresh woody scents and sweet floral fragrances filled the air, banishing the rotten stench of the Graydig.

Aunty Connie burst back into the room, panting, her hair sticking up. "I finally managed to turn off the water.

Oh! What happened to the flood?" she said, looking around the hall.

Ananya quickly grabbed a mop that was propped against the wall. "All sorted! It wasn't that bad in the end."

"Really?" Aunty Connie stared at them, amazed.

Tamzin sat back and nodded, smiling weakly.

"It looked much worse than it was," said Maya.

Aunty Connie sighed. "Well, that's a relief. Thank goodness you girls are always here to save the day."

Aunty Connie fetched the director, and the girls started their audition again. This time, they made it all the way through their song. It felt as though the excitement of battling the Graydig had given their performance an extra electric energy, and when they finished, the director and Aunty Connie gave them a standing ovation.

Jenny looked proudly at her friends.

"That was amazing," said the director. "How would you girls like to be on the programme?"

"You mean we're in?" asked Jenny.

The director smiled. "Not just in the show – you're going to open the fair."

Jenny punched the air and the girls all cheered.

"Just one thing," said the director over their squeals of excitement. "What's your band's name?"

"Er . . ." Jenny looked at Maya and Ananya in panic. They hadn't had a chance to come up with a name yet!

Jenny desperately glanced around the room for inspiration and her eyes fell on a poster for the Spellcroft Fair. "Spellcasters?" she said quickly.

Maya gave her the thumbs up, Tamzin nodded and Ananya grinned.

"I love it!" said Aunty Connie.

The director smiled. "Sounds great! Well, all right, Spellcasters, see you at the fair!"

As soon as Aunty Connie had walked the director out, Jenny and her friends gathered around Tamzin.

"That was incredible, Tamzin," said Maya.

"How did you know what to do?" asked Ananya.

"And what was that word you said?" asked Jenny. "*Idan?*"

"It's Yoruba, the language my ancestors spoke. My mum and I looked it up online last night and it means 'magic'," explained Tamzin. "I found it on an inscription inside my ring that I'd never noticed before." She took off her ring to show them. "My mum told me about a family legend which says that the ring used to belong to a mythical healer called Gang Gang Sarah, who came from West Africa and flew on the winds to the Caribbean."

"Wow," said Maya. "So your magical powers come from your ancestors, and your spells work when you use the word for magic written on your talisman, same as mine. That must be the key!"

"When I said the spells, it felt as though my ancestors were by my side, guiding me." Tamzin's eyes shone as she spoke. "I felt so powerful."

"The Graydig is getting stronger too,

though," said Maya gravely. "We could have been electrocuted!"

Ananya nodded in agreement. "Me and Jenny need to find our spells, fast!"

CHAPTER SEVEN

Jenny woke the next morning to find the kitchen a hive of activity. The Spellcroft Fair was only a day away. Gong Gong was chopping onions as fast as any chef. Diced carrots and cubes of potato were heaped in bowls, and there was a mound of minced lamb and onions, cooked with spices.

"Por Por, can I ask you about my bracelet?" said Jenny. She'd tried talking to her grandparents the night before, but they'd been too busy prepping. Jenny wondered if they'd even slept at all.

"Not now, Jenny." Por Por pummelled a ball of dough. Flour puffed into the air, dusting her hair and face and making Jenny sneeze. "We have hundreds of curry puffs to bake for our stall." She thumped the dough with a rolling pin.

"You love extra spicy?" Gong Gong spooned more curry powder into the lamb mix, winking at Jenny. Delicious smells filled the room.

"Mmm, yum!" Jenny's mouth
watered. Curry puffs were her favourite
Malaysian snack. The crisp pastry
contained a delicious, spicy mix of meat
and vegetables.

"You have time to cut out a few
circles?" Por Por asked, handing her a

rice bowl to use as a pastry cutter.

She showed Jenny how to spoon the right amount of filling into the pastry circle, fold the pastry, and crimp the edge with her finger and thumb.

"Por Por, can I ask you about my bracelet?" Jenny tried again.

"Of course, *bao-beh*, what about it?" Por Por said, sniffing. "What's that smell?" An acrid burning smell filled the kitchen.

"*Aiyo, aiyo!*" shouted Gong Gong as the smoke alarm went off. The baking paper on a tray of curry puffs had caught fire on the stove. He quickly threw a cup of water on it.

Jenny sighed. Her grandparents would be too busy to talk to her about her bracelet until the fair was over. She hoped Ananya was having more luck.

At morning break, Ananya rushed towards the others. "Such a cool story about my hairclip. My mum showed me the inscription – it was there all along." She undid the hairclip and showed them the tiny engraving on the underside. "*Jādū* means 'magic' in Punjabi!"

"Wow!" said Maya.

"Last night, my mum said her nani used to tell her stories about someone in their family, generations back, who could make things move with her mind and make wishes come true!" said Ananya. "A magical wishing tree in India gave her the power."

"I bet your hairclip used to belong to her," said Tamzin.

"Maybe," said Ananya. "I haven't had a chance to try out any spells because my mum made me go to bed. But I have a good feeling about this."

Jenny was happy that Ananya had found the key to her magic, but she felt left out. She was the one who had noticed their glowing talismans that fateful day at the building site. She was the one who had brought them all together. But she was the only one not to have unlocked her powers. She couldn't help feeling a pang of disappointment.

Ananya looked at her, as though sensing her pain. "Don't worry, Jenny. We'll help you figure this out. You left your body and went down into the sinkhole on your first day of school. Maybe there's something about that place that activates your magic?"

The bell rang, signalling the end of break.

"Let's meet in the library at lunchtime," said Tamzin. "We can do some research into local history."

"We'll help you find your magic again," said Maya, putting her arm around Jenny's shoulders.

Tamzin and Maya had to queue for school dinners, but Jenny and Ananya ate their packed lunches quickly and got to the library first.

The librarian, Mrs Khan, was putting books away when they arrived. "Ananya, I haven't seen you for a while! You came to see me every day at the beginning of term, but it's been a while since we've had one of our chats.

How are you doing?"

Ananya looked a bit embarrassed but smiled broadly at Mrs Khan. "I'm good, thanks. Much better now I'm in a band! We're performing at the Spellcroft Fair. We're actually here to look for books on the history of the local area though – for a project."

"Well, this area is steeped in rich history, girls," said the librarian. "I wish I could stay and help you, but I'm already a few minutes late for our staff meeting."

"Is it OK if we stay in the library?" asked Ananya. "To look stuff up."

"Of course you can!" Mrs Khan

showed them to the local history section. "And there are the computers too, if you want to do any research online."

When Mrs Khan had left, Jenny wandered over to her desk and noticed a copy of the local newspaper. The headline made her stomach flip. *"TENSIONS RISE – SPELLCROFT PROTESTS"*. Jenny quickly scanned the article. *"According to a Spellcroft councillor, building work is set to recommence soon, and the final decision on the development will be made next week."*

Oh no, thought Jenny. *That doesn't*

sound good for The Oaks. The decision would upset a lot of people, which was exactly what the Graydig wanted.

"Did you find anything?" asked Tamzin as she walked in with Maya.

"This looks interesting," Ananya said, holding up an old book, its pages yellowed with age. The Spellcasters crowded round.

"*A History of Spellcroft*," Jenny said, reading the title.

"Oh wow, look at these old photos!" Maya carefully turned the pages to reveal a series of faded sepia photos of Spellcroft long ago, with boys in flat caps and girls in white smocks, printed on thick, shiny paper.

"Looks like the Bubble Tea Café used to be a butcher's," said Tamzin.

"Isn't this where The Oaks is now?" asked Jenny, turning the page to reveal a photo of a field with a small oak tree in the centre.

Ananya read the introduction.

"Historians believe there was an ancient dwelling in the land known as Spell Croft, predating the arrival of the Romans. Foundations of stone buildings from the time of the Celts have been found in the area. Local legend says that the village was built on the path of a magical ley line, near the

oak woods, *where Celtic druids would conduct their ceremonies.*"

"What's a ley line?" asked Tamzin.

"I don't know," said Jenny. "But I know how we can find out." She quickly searched for "ley line" on the library computer, and her eyes grew wide.

"*Ley lines are a theory that important spiritual monuments around the world are joined together by straight lines. Those lines have powerful energy, like the dragon lines in Chinese feng shui,*" read Tamzin over her shoulder.

"Right before the sinkhole opened, I saw lines of light streaking through the ground, and there was a burst of light by the building site," said Jenny. "What if the drilling disturbed the magical ley line energy, which somehow activated the ancient magic inside our jewellery?"

"So magic from our ancestors has been turned on by the ley line and now we have the power!" said Tamzin excitedly. "But so does the Graydig . . ."

She leaned over Ananya's shoulder to read more. "*There is a charming myth behind the name of the village, Spell Croft. A croft in ancient Britannia was an enclosed field. A spell was a powerful incantation or story, used by the druids to contain bad spirits.*"

She turned the page and read further. "*Legend tells us that in medieval times, there was an evil spirit that caused trouble for the peace-loving villagers. Fresh milk went sour and sheep died for no reason—*"

"This sounds like the Graydig!" Maya interjected.

Tamzin carried on. "*. . . until a group of young women cast a spell, using Celtic runes to channel the magical power of their ancestors. They defeated the spirit, and in honour of their magic, the area was named Spell Croft.*"

Jenny's jaw dropped as she was stunned into silence.

"So this place has always been really magical," said Ananya.

"The medieval women used spells to defeat the Graydig," said Jenny, finding her voice. "Now that it has been released again, we can use our own spells in the same way!"

"Let's see if we can find out anything more about those girls," said Tamzin. As the girls scanned the bookshelves, Jenny hummed the oak tree song. The others started humming too.

Suddenly, Jenny felt the ground tremble.

What was that? Jenny pressed her feet firmly into the ground.

A book flew off the top shelf, landing on the floor with a thump.

"Did you feel that?" Ananya asked anxiously. "It felt like an earthquake. We had one when we were on holiday in India once."

The floor trembled harder. Books flew off the shaking shelves and rained down on the girls.

"Everyone – under the table!" shouted Maya.

The girls dived for cover. Outside, the wind howled and rattled the windowpanes until one of the windows swung wide open. A cloud of green mist curled into the room.

"It's the Graydig!" cried Jenny, holding her nose against the stench. The mist was hazy at first, but thickened until the library was shrouded in a dense fog.

Jenny gasped as a tall, hooded figure emerged from the fog, wrapped in a dark cloak that seemed to be made of decayed leaves. Out of its hood, where a face should be, billowed more clouds of the stinky mist.

Jenny's heart pounded in her chest. If this was the Graydig, it had gained enough strength to take on a physical form. It was no longer just a voice.

The figure raised its arms, and a fierce

gale whipped round the library. Books were swept off the shelves and flew around the room like missiles.

The Spellcasters watched in horror as the table they were crouched under began to shake, rocking backwards and forwards on its legs.

BANG!

The table tipped over and a gust of wind smashed it against the opposite wall. Jenny looked wildly around at the others, hoping to see a glow of magic. But no one's talisman was even flickering. They were all too scared.

"You should have heeded my warnings," a calm, matter-of-fact voice croaked from the depths of the hood. The Graydig loomed over them. "You think you can stop me? A bunch of weak children? Do not meddle with forces you do not understand. This is your last warning."

The Graydig's cloak billowed around it and then it was gone – whooshing through the window and out into the sky, drawing the green smoke with it. The wind died down immediately and the ground stopped shaking.

The girls stayed crouched on the floor as the last of the mist dissipated.

Jenny's heart sank as she looked at the destruction left in the Graydig's wake.

Amazingly, no one was hurt, but the library was completely trashed – chairs were upturned, shelves were out of place and books were strewn on every possible surface. Mrs Khan would be back soon, and she would think they had done it.

The others stood up shakily.

"How are we going to put everything back?" said Maya, staring around her in shock. "So much for being brave. I didn't even try and use my magic."

"Me neither," said Tamzin. "No wonder the Graydig thinks we're just a bunch of weaklings."

Ananya stuck her hands on her hips

and pulled her shoulders back. "The Graydig is going to wish it had never met us." She put a hand on her hairclip decisively and it glowed brightly.

"Jādū, *right these things gone wrong, Ancient powers, make me strong.*"

Ananya stood in front of a bookcase that had fallen over, frowning in concentration.

The bookcase trembled and lifted up. Ananya held her hands out in front of her, palms facing outwards. The others stared in astonishment as the bookcase turned upright and returned to its place by the wall. Ananya repeated the same magic until all the bookcases were in place. Then she closed her eyes and spread her arms out towards the books on the floor.

"Jādū *rights what evil wrongs,*
   Ancient powers, put this back where
it belongs."

The other girls watched, open-mouthed, as the books rose in the air. Pages rustled back into position; covers snapped shut. The books hovered in the air, then danced back to their shelves, lined up neatly in rows.

"Incredible – they're even in alphabetical order!" said Jenny.

Ananya stood back and the spell was broken. "It worked! The magic felt so much stronger this time – like I was in control. I concentrated hard on wishing for what I wanted to happen, and I could feel my ancestors helping me."

"That was amazing!" said Maya.

"Your magic is really powerful," said Tamzin.

"Shapeshifting and healing magic are cool too." Ananya shrugged, beaming with pride.

Jenny listened enviously as her friends talked about their powers. She twisted the bracelet on her wrist. She hadn't found any inscription on it, and it hadn't glowed since that first day at the building site. The thought of being powerless against the Graydig riddled her with nerves.

The Graydig was getting stronger – and, for some reason, it saw the girls as a threat. First the frogs, then the graffiti and the flood. And now the library. They had to stop it before someone got seriously hurt.

"Hi, girls,' said Mrs Khan, walking back into the library. "Did you find what you were looking for?"

"I'd like to take this book out, please," said Jenny, handing Mrs Khan *A History of Spellcroft*.

Mrs Khan entered it into the computer and beamed at Jenny. "I don't think I've read this one. Enjoy!"

I'm going to study this book cover to cover, thought Jenny, putting the history book carefully in her bag. There had to be a clue in it somewhere for defeating the Graydig. And without magical powers to help her, books were her only hope.

CHAPTER EIGHT

The girls agreed to meet at The Oaks after school to rehearse, but there was an even bigger crowd in front of the building site when they got there.

Protestors were shouting, punching the air and shaking placards at each other.

"People, not profits! Hands off our

community centre!" chanted one group, holding posters of children playing in The Oaks garden.

"Boost our economy! Develop Spellcroft Street!" shouted another group. Their posters showed a big shopping complex surrounded by modern glass buildings on either side.

Green mist rose, reeking of sulphur, and surrounded the protestors – though they seemed oblivious to it. Someone threw a plastic drink bottle into the crowd, causing more chaos.

"Look at that." Tamzin pointed to the trees nearest the sinkhole. Their leaves drooped under the heavy mist.

"The Graydig's killing the trees!" gasped Ananya.

"Can't you save them, Tamzin – like you saved the plants in the hall?" Jenny asked.

"I can try," Tamzin replied. She touched her ring and red light flooded her face. The spell flowed easily:

"Idan, *make my talisman glow,*
Ancient powers, let healing flow."

Tamzin put her hand on the trunk of a horse chestnut tree, its spiky pods shrivelled and black. Her ring glowed brighter. As the spell's magic

worked, the leaves started to uncurl. The spiky cases plumped out and turned bright green. Some split open and shiny brown conkers plopped out.

Next, Tamzin turned to a holly bush. Its leaves were turning yellow. She touched them and concentrated hard. Under Tamzin's magic, the holly leaves turned a deep green and bright red berries popped up all over the bush.

Tamzin moved to a copper birch tree nearest the sinkhole. Dead leaves were piled on the ground beneath it and its branches were covered in green slime.

Tamzin concentrated hard, casting her spell, but eventually she fell back, exhausted. "I'm sorry. This one is too far gone. I don't think it can be saved."

"The birch is nearest to the Graydig's lair," said Jenny. "Maybe its power is too strong here."

"Come and sit down," Maya said to Tamzin, leading her over to the front steps of The Oaks, with Ananya and Jenny close behind.

"It's no use." Tamzin's forehead was shiny with sweat. "What if the Graydig is right and we can't stop it?"

Jenny leaned in, struggling to hear Tamzin over the shouting of the protestors. "What do you mean?"

"Think of all the damage it did in the library. We were lucky not to get hurt. If the Graydig gets more powerful, we might not be so lucky next time."

Jenny heard police sirens wailing in the distance and another plastic bottle bounced on to the pavement nearby. She could feel a tight ball of frustration growing inside her. "But we can't let the Graydig win."

Tendrils of foul green mist wafted over to where the girls were sitting, curling round their trainers, snaking up their legs.

"There's not much we can do, just the three of us." Ananya crossed her arms and looked pointedly at Jenny.

"What's that supposed to mean?" asked Jenny.

Ananya shook her head. "Nothing."

"No, go on, just say what you want to say," Jenny insisted.

"It's just that you're the only one who hasn't managed to use her powers yet. You could be helping us stop the Graydig, but you've done nothing."

Tears stung Jenny's eyes.

"I've been trying to—" Jenny began.

"All I wanted was to fit in at school and steer clear of drama – and drama is all I've got being friends with you lot!" Ananya scowled. "I wish I'd never even joined the band."

"What?" Jenny's face flamed with anger, like someone had punched her. "I can't believe you just said that."

Maya gasped. "Ananya, you don't mean it!"

Ananya shrugged.

"Maybe we should just stop," Tamzin interrupted, shaking her head. "I don't want anyone to get hurt. Let's not perform at the fair tomorrow."

"But what about the band?" Maya said, looking hurt.

"The four of us hanging out together seems to wind the Graydig up," said Tamzin. "Maybe if we stay away from each other, it will leave us all alone."

"Aunty Connie is counting on us," said Jenny. "The Oaks will shut down if the fair isn't a success. We have to help save the community centre."

"I'm sorry," Tamzin said. She rubbed her eyes. "I just need a break."

"Listen, we can't give up," said Jenny. "The Graydig won't stop until it destroys everything we care about."

"How do you know what the Graydig's thinking? I don't care any more. I'm going home," said Ananya. "My parents would worry if they knew I was here, anyway."

"Yeah, I'm going home too – alone," said Maya, shooting Tamzin an angry look. She turned on her heel and stalked off without looking back. Ananya walked off in the opposite direction.

"This is what the Graydig wants," said Jenny. "For us to fall out. It feeds on discord."

Tamzin stood up and shook her head. "Sorry, Jenny, I just think we all need some space. This is for the best."

Jenny stood, watching Tamzin walk off too, leaving her all alone.

A gust of green mist circled around her and the Graydig's dead, flat voice whispered in her ear. *Don't say you're surprised. You knew it wouldn't last. They never really wanted to be your friends. It's all been too good to be true.*

"No! You're lying," said Jenny out loud, but she didn't believe it.

Ananya's words echoed in Jenny's mind as she pushed past the angry mass of protestors swarming down the street. When Por Por opened the door to

their flat, Jenny
rushed into her
arms, breathing
in her comforting
lavender scent.

"Oh, Por! I
hate it here!" she
sobbed.

"What's wrong,
bao-beh? *Jenny-
ah*, tell me." Por Por patted Jenny's
back while she cried and cried. Por
Por handed her a tissue. "I'll get you a
snack." She fetched a glass of mango
juice and a freshly baked curry puff.
"Come. Tell me what happened."

Jenny sipped the sweet juice. "I was wrong to think I'd have friends here. I don't fit in anywhere."

Por Por sighed. "Oh, *Jenny-ah*. Friendship can be difficult. You do not always want the same thing as your friend. You want to do this, they want to do that. When I was a schoolgirl, back in Malaysia . . ."

Jenny smiled through her tears. She couldn't imagine Por Por as a young girl!

Por Por nudged her. "Yes, yes, your Por was young once. I remember fighting with my good friend, Jackie, when I was at high school in Batu

Pahat. She say, let's go to waterfall. But the next day is maths exam. I want to study. She got so angry. We fight, but she stay behind. You know what happened in the end?"

"What happened?" Jenny asked.

"Jackie achieve high mark in the exam, same as me. So she say 'thank you'. I was right."

Jenny gave a wobbly laugh. "Por, really? You'd rather revise for a maths exam than swim in a waterfall?"

"*Aiya*, I was a very good student. Jenny, you must have hope. Everything will work out fine. Have hope. Eh – look." Por Por patted her bracelet.

"There's a hidden message from our ancestor, right here on your bracelet. Your ancestors are always looking out for you."

"What do you mean?" Jenny frowned, puzzled. She hadn't seen any message, no matter how hard she'd looked.

Por Por slipped the bracelet off Jenny's wrist and held it up to the window. "See? The Mandarin characters for 'magic'. *Mófă.*"

On the inside of the bracelet was a faint inscription. It could only be seen with the light shining through at a very particular angle.

"*Mófǎ*," whispered Jenny.

Por Por held her tightly. "You know, Jenny, I will always be here, looking out for you. Just like the spirit of my Por Por is always here for me. We Chinese believe the spirits of our ancestors never leave us. They are always close, helping us live a good life. So we say thanks to them by lighting a joss stick. We remember our loved ones who have passed away."

"But why does the bracelet say 'magic'?" asked Jenny.

Por Por patted her back. "Eh, you know, in our family, one of our ancestors was a shaman, a Wu."

"What's a Wu?" Jenny asked.

"A Wu is a female shaman who speaks to the spirit world. She can astral project – magically leave her body to travel through space and time," Por Por explained.

That's what I did when I went down into the sinkhole! thought Jenny.

"It is said that your jade bracelet is passed down from that Wu," said Por Por. "I don't know if it has magical powers, but they say that every few generations there is a Wu."

Suddenly full of energy, Jenny jumped up.

"Thanks, Por Por!" she said, giving

her grandmother a hug. "I feel much better now." She had to try the spell – there was no more time to waste!

CHAPTER NINE

Jenny shut her door and sat on her bed, heart pounding. She looked at the clock – it was five past four. She switched on her bedside lamp and held her bracelet up to the light again. *Mófǎ.*

I allowed my fear of the Graydig to become greater than my belief in myself, thought Jenny. She had let it scare her and make her feel worthless.

But she remembered the other voice
that had spoken to her in the sinkhole.
It had told her to fight, not to give up.
*My ancestors have been with me all
along; I just couldn't see it!*

Jenny's wrist felt hot. Her bracelet
was glowing a bright green, now clearly
showing the markings of the Chinese
characters for 'magic'.

Jenny sat cross-legged and
concentrated hard, breathing in and out
slowly, thinking about her ancestors,
about all the women who had worn
the jade bracelet throughout the years.
It felt as though they were in the

room with her, encouraging her. Jenny
clutched her bracelet and the words of
her spell came to her.

"Mófǎ, *take me to another land,*
Ancient powers, help me understand!"

Jenny's face fizzed with the bubbles-up-
the-nose feeling. Her whole head was
tingling, aching with pressure.

Suddenly, something inside her
lurched . . .

And she was floating above her body.

Jenny rose up to the ceiling. This time,
she knew what to expect. Jenny gazed
at the cracks in the paint and the fine

threads of cobwebs hanging from the
corners. The window was open.

I want to go outside.

As soon as the thought entered her
mind, she was floating out of the
window. She was rising higher and

higher until she could see the whole of
Spellcroft Street spread below like a
carpet. At one end was The Oaks, with
the oak tree at the back of the grass
lawn. Next to it, the sinkhole looked
like a small pothole from up high, with

green smoke curling out. The crowd of demonstrators was frozen in time. The Graydig had caught them in its toxic cloud of negativity and was feeding off their anger.

If you're listening, ancestors, thought Jenny, *please show me how to defeat the Graydig.*

Out of nowhere, a silvery path of light appeared, and she whooshed upwards into the clouds. Spellcroft Street disappeared, and soon the earth was a green and blue planet far below Jenny. All around her burned white-hot stars, and she tingled with wonder.

Visions passed in front of her, like on

a cinema screen. There were her mum and dad, saying goodbye to her at the airport in Bangkok. Next, she saw Por Por, her hair black, pushing an old-fashioned pushchair with a baby in it. Running ahead was an older girl of about eleven. Jenny recognised Mum and Aunty Connie from old photos.

It was like the history of Jenny's family was winding backwards, as she travelled further and further back in time.

Jenny saw an even younger Por Por, her hair in an updo, the jade bracelet on her arm. She stood on the deck of an ocean liner, waving goodbye to Jenny's

great-grandmother,
an old-fashioned
Chinese woman on the
dock, dressed in a trouser
suit.

Then Por Por was a little girl, hair in
bunches, riding on the back of a bicycle
with her mother, who was wearing the
bracelet this time. She rode into a forest

of trees with green leaves and streaks running down their trunks. Jenny's great-grandmother slashed the bark of the tree and used a bucket to catch the sap. They set buckets of stinky rubber sap out to dry in the sun.

Jenny travelled further back in time.

Another Chinese girl was in a paddy field. A hailstorm had damaged the rice crop, followed by a drought. The plants were brown and shrivelled. People were hungry. The girl travelled with her parents in a horse and cart, and then on a steamboat. They arrived in a lush green tropical country – Malaysia. The girl's mother gave her the jade bracelet.

Jenny whooshed past years and years, all the way to ancient times. She saw a young woman standing on top of a mountain. She wore a headdress of bones and feathers. Her pink silk grown had bell-shaped sleeves that trailed to the ground.

The woman faced a dragon that swooped across the mountain range, flapping its wings angrily. It wasn't kind and friendly, like Chinese dragons normally are. Its eyes sparked red with rage. As it screeched, its fiery breath burned trees and scorched the grass. The sulphurous stench was familiar and, somehow, Jenny knew an evil spirit like the Graydig had possessed this dragon too.

This young woman wasn't afraid. She glared fiercely at the dragon, holding her arms up, a green ring of light glowing brightly on her wrist. It was the very same jade bracelet that was around Jenny's wrist now. The woman looked tiny compared to the angry dragon circling the mountain top like a predator. Further down the mountain, frightened villagers had grabbed their children and were hiding behind rocks and bushes.

Jenny remembered Por Por's words. *Our ancestor is a shaman, a Wu . . .*

The Wu began to dance, twirling one way and then the other. Her trailing skirts and sleeves swirled, making patterns in the air. She lifted her arms, twisting and spinning faster. Jenny caught glimpses of the jade bracelet burning brightly through the swirling silk.

The Wu began to sing in a Chinese dialect. Her voice sounded clear and strong, calming the dragon. And even though Jenny did not speak that dialect, she could understand her ancestor's words. Maybe the memory of that language had been passed down to her, in her cells.

"Mófǎ *fills me with might,*
Ancient powers, help me fight."

The dragon stopped beating its wings
and hovered above the Wu's head. The
dragon opened its mouth to roar, and
only a small puff of smoke curled out.
The scorching fire had been quenched
by the Wu's magic. The red glow in the
dragon's eyes faded to a pale gold.

The dragon landed on the mountain
top and settled down in front of the
Wu, curling up by her feet like a giant
dog. The Wu stepped forward and
stroked the dragon's scaly head.

Jenny cheered and clapped. "Yes!"

The local villagers left their hiding places and rushed back up the mountain, beating their gongs and drums and ringing bells. The evil spirit had been driven out of the dragon, and they were safe again.

The shaman glanced up at Jenny, as if she could see her. And she smiled.

Jenny was filled with a powerful confidence. Jenny's ancestor, the shaman, had used her song to drive the evil spirit from the dragon.

Could the power of song defeat the Graydig too?

It was time to go back.

CHAPTER TEN

Jenny was whooshing, fast as light, along the silver path back to her body. She snapped her eyes open and glanced at the clock. The hands hadn't moved. It was still five past four. Time had stopped, like that first day by the sinkhole.

The Graydig had been trying to break

up the Spellcasters ever since they'd formed the band. Maybe it was because it didn't want them to perform together. Maybe it was scared of them.

"I'm going out," Jenny called to Por Por. "To see my friends."

Maya lived in Spellcroft Towers, which was nearest to Jenny's flat. Jenny ran all the way there and nervously waited for the lift. The Graydig's words were still ringing in her ears. *Is this friendship too good to be true?*

Finally, a woman with gold earrings and a cloud of dark curly hair opened the door. The hallway behind her was crowded with coats and shoes, and the walls were crammed with family photos. Jenny smiled. "Hello. I'm Jenny, Maya's friend. Is Maya in?"

"Hello, Jenny. Maya has told me all about you – and your band! I'm Maya's mum. It's lovely to meet you at last. Maya!" She went down the hallway, knocked on a door and said something in Arabic. Then she went into the kitchen.

The door opened and Maya appeared in the hallway, looking sheepish. "Hi, Jenny. About earlier . . ." she began.

"Never mind about that," Jenny said in a low voice. "Guess what? I did a spell that worked!"

Maya grinned, wide-eyed. "Really?! That's brilliant!"

"I think I know how we can defeat the Graydig," Jenny said. "But we need to put the band back together."

"Let's go and tell Tamzin," said Maya. "She texted me – I know she's feeling bad about what happened. Mum, can we go out?"

"Wait – I can't let a guest leave without food!" Maya's mum rushed out of the kitchen, thrusting a family-sized box of chocolate biscuits into her hands. "Here. Share these with your friends."

"Thank you!" said the girls.

Tamzin lived in a row of terraced houses not far from Maya. Jenny rang the doorbell. A cello arpeggio drifted out of an upstairs window. Downstairs, scales rang out from a piano.

A teenage girl with a silk scarf round her afro answered the door. "Oh, hi, Maya – Tamzin's practising. Go on up."

"Thanks, Rachel!" Maya led the way upstairs. She rapped on a door covered with glittery letters that spelled out "Tamzin". The cello playing stopped and the door opened.

"Oh, I'm so glad you're both here—"

Tamzin began when she saw them.

Maya interrupted. "Guess what?"

"I know how to use my magic!" Jenny burst out.

"That's great!" Tamzin said, beaming. "I'm really sorry about earlier. I don't know what came over us."

"I felt so angry out there," said Maya. "I don't know why."

"It was the Graydig; that's what it does," Jenny said, shrugging. "It stirs up anger and sets people against each other. That's why we fell out."

"We need to tell Ananya," said Tamzin. "I know where she lives."

They ran all the way to an imposing

three-storey house at the far end of Spellcroft Street, with a neat lawn, palm trees in pots and a slate-chipped path. The door was a glossy black, with a brass lion knocker.

"Whoa!" said Jenny. Ananya's house was much bigger than Por Por's flat.

Maya rapped smartly, and the sound echoed. The door opened, and Ananya's older brother appeared, carrying a toddler, who waved at them.

"Hiya," Maya said, waving back. "Can we see Ananya, please?"

"Come in; I'll get her." Ananya's brother let them into the black-and-white tiled hall and put the toddler down before walking up the stairs.

"Must be one of Ananya's little cousins. So cute," Tamzin said to Jenny.

Jenny glanced at the antique Indian furniture and studio portraits of Ananya and her family. A delicious spicy smell drifted out from the back, and voices chatted in a room nearby.

The toddler grabbed a plastic fire engine, pressed a button and the siren blared out. He zoomed it about the hall, then said, "Nanya, Nanya!"

Ananya came down the wooden staircase and stiffened when she saw the girls in the hall.

"I'm so glad you're here," Ananya

said quickly.
"I don't know
what came
over me, but I
am so—"
"Jenny's
magic
worked!"
Maya
whispered, interrupting Ananya.

Ananya ran the rest of the way down
the stairs and hugged Jenny. "Yeah?"

Jenny nodded, suddenly feeling self-
conscious.

"I feel soooo bad," said Ananya. "I
don't know what made me say such

cruel things. I didn't mean any of it."

Jenny bit her lip. "And I'm sorry, for being so – so pushy."

"Jenny, you're the one that got us all together and I'm so grateful. You're the new girl but you made me feel like I belonged."

Jenny felt warm inside. She held her jade bracelet up to the sunlight. "See this Chinese inscription? My grandmother said it means 'magic'. Once my Por Por taught me the word, I was able to find my spell. And I astral projected!"

"What does that mean?" asked Tamzin, looking confused.

"It's the same thing that happened at the building site. I left my body and I went to ancient China!"

"So you travelled through space and time," said Ananya, looking impressed.

Jenny nodded. "I asked for help from all of my ancestors and saw a glimpse into their lives. One of them – a female shaman, the Wu – defeated a dragon who was disturbing her village. It was possessed with an evil spirit, like the Graydig. The Wu sang a spell and the evil spirit left the dragon."

Tamzin gasped. "So you think you could summon a magic spell to defeat the Graydig?"

"At least, that's what I think the Wu was telling me," said Jenny.

"So the Graydig used its magic to try and break us up . . ." said Tamzin. "And you think we should sing at the fair to lure it out into the open?"

"And then Jenny will sing a spell to defeat it!" Maya karate-chopped the air.

Ananya nodded. "You know, it might just work."

"Ananya, dear." A woman in a paisley silk dress opened the door to the kitchen. "Aunty Meena brought samosas. You like samosas, girls?"

"Mmm, thank you, Aunty," said Tamzin, licking her lips.

"I brought chocolate biscuits too."
Maya waved the box from her mum.

The girls went into the kitchen
and tucked into spicy samosas and
chocolate biscuits with Ananya's family.

Afterwards, they all went upstairs to
Ananya's bedroom. They all sat on the
big double bed and talked for hours.

"Well, now we're all friends again, I
feel like this is the perfect time to give
you these!" Tamzin handed them each a
friendship bracelet. "Look at what they
say."

Jenny looked down and saw that
the bracelet read "SPELLCASTERS"
in colourful letters and was strung

together with silver, red, green and gold beads that represented the four magic talismans. It sat perfectly above Jenny's jade bracelet.

Jenny blinked the tears away from her eyes. "Tamzin, I don't know what to say. Thank you."

Jenny beamed at her fellow Spellcasters. The evil spirit had been wrong. These girls were her real friends, and she knew that together, they could defeat anything.

CHAPTER ELEVEN

Sunlight peeked through the curtains. The day of the Spellcroft Fair had finally arrived. Jenny jumped out of bed, full of nervous energy.

Delicious smells filled the flat. Por Por and Gong Gong were baking the final batch of curry puffs. Boxes labelled 'Vegetarian', 'Lamb' and 'Chicken' were stacked up, ready to take to The Oaks.

Por Por waved her phone at Jenny. "She is up – you want to talk?" She handed the phone over. "Mum wants you."

Jenny took Por Por's mobile and grinned at her mum and dad's smiling faces on the screen.

"Good luck for your performance, my darling," said Mum. "We'll be watching the livestream." Mum swiped her eyes.

"*Aiya*, middle of the night for you." Por Por tutted. "Must sleep."

"It's our baby's first public performance. We can't miss it." Dad blew Jenny a kiss.

"Love you, Mum and Dad!" If only today were as easy as just performing in front of a crowd at the fair. Jenny felt sure, deep in her bones, that the Graydig wouldn't be able to resist turning up to try and ruin the fair. But the Spellcasters would be waiting.

After breakfast, Jenny and her family headed for The Oaks. A queue for the fair snaked down the street, and there was already a thick green fog creeping up to obscure the sun. The tape cordoning off the sinkhole was green with mould. All the nearby trees, even the ones Tamzin had healed the day before, were shrivelled and dying.

Some people held their noses or pressed tissues to their faces to mask the sulphurous reek drifting on the breeze.

"Smells like the sinkhole disrupted the sewage pipes," said Gong Gong. He kissed Jenny goodbye and left to fetch the rest of the curry puffs.

"Too many chemicals," said Por Por, shaking her head. "Bad for the trees."

But Jenny knew the mould wasn't being caused by chemicals or sewage. It was the Graydig's evil.

Maya, Tamzin and Ananya were waiting for Jenny by the side entrance and Aunty Connie's colleague showed them through to the garden and the stage where they would perform. Around the perimeter were food stalls, all strung with bunting and flags from around the world, heaving under the weight of all the tasty treats.

Tamzin examined the great oak tree in the heart of the garden. Its tall branches were spread out and its leaves were still green.

"The Celts believed that oak trees were magical. They must be right. It's the only tree unaffected by the Graydig," said Tamzin sadly.

Aunty Connie bustled over. "Come on, girls – the people from the council have arrived; it's time to open the fair."

The Spellcasters climbed on to the stage behind Connie and she grabbed the microphone. Behind her, a red satin ribbon tied in a huge bow was strung up on stage supports. The small crowd in front of the stage started to clap.

"Welcome, everyone, to the Spellcroft—" There was a squeal of feedback from the microphone. "—FAIR!" Aunty Connie's voice boomed out, making everyone jump. "Oops, sorry! First, I must apologise for the mess at the building site and the horrible smell. In the meantime, let's focus on the treats we have in store for you today." Her face brightened. "A day of live music from local bands, like the Spellcasters here . . ."

The girls whooped and the crowd clapped, but it was a muted response. The terrible smell was getting stronger and stronger. It made Jenny feel sick to her stomach.

Aunty Connie bravely carried on. "Delicious street food from around the world. A tombola, art and crafts, a bouncy castle . . ."

People in the crowd began to cough, and others drifted away. Soon, people were rushing inside, covering their mouths.

"The Oaks community centre is . . .

the beating heart of the local area." Aunty Connie looked around desperately.

The garden was now deserted. She coughed and turned to the Spellcasters, looking defeated. "Well, this hasn't gone quite to plan."

"You go inside, Aunty Connie," said Jenny. "We'll pack up and follow you in."

Aunty Connie nodded and, coughing, ran inside the centre.

"The Graydig is close; I can feel it," whispered Maya.

"I can smell it," said Tamzin.

Ananya gasped. "Look!"

A tall figure stalked through the mist towards the girls. Its floor-length cloak was covered with mud and mulched-up leaves. Moss and twigs trailed behind, and a cavernous hood covered its face. The Graydig!

The hood of the cloak swivelled from side to side, two dark green eyes shining from somewhere deep inside. "You did not heed my warning." Its flat, dead voice sent a chill down Jenny's spine and made the hairs on the back of her neck stand up.

The Graydig raised its arms, casting the entire garden into shadow.

A freezing gust of wind howled,

upturning tables, ripping at the stalls, spilling drinks and crushing food.

"Now you will see that I am too strong for you."

The sleeves of the cloak lifted in the air and the stalls were carried away by the gale.

The girls crouched to shield themselves from the flying debris and then Maya bravely stumbled to her feet. She held up her necklace and chanted a spell.

"Sehr *swirling through the air,*
Ancient powers, turn me into a bear."

Her necklace glowed bright silver. Maya squeezed her eyes shut and went very still.

"Whoa, Maya," Tamzin breathed in awe as Maya shapeshifted into a huge brown bear. Maya the bear stood on her hind legs, ten feet tall. She let out a guttural growl, showing her fearsome teeth, and launched herself at the Graydig. She swiped at the Graydig's robe with sharp claws.

"A bear? Hah! You can't stop me!" the

Graydig hissed. It thrust out an arm and green smoke billowed from the sleeve, forming a shield of magical light.

The bear crashed into the shield and was thrown to one side. Maya shapeshifted back into a human and curled in a ball on the ground, yelping with pain.

Ananya stepped forward, looking fierce. "No one hurts my friend and gets away with it!" She touched her hairclip and it glowed golden, like the sun. She wasted no time in casting her spell.

"Jādū *grants my every wish,*
Ancient powers, help me vanquish."

Frowning with concentration, Ananya focused on a heavy picnic table.

The table trembled and lifted ten centimetres off the ground. Then twenty centimetres, then fifty.

Jenny gasped in astonishment as she saw the heavy object rise high in the air and then go crashing down towards the Graydig. But the Graydig threw up its arms again, smashing the table in mid-air. The wooden legs of the table flew through the air like missiles and came crashing down, followed by the tabletop.

Ananya had to dive off the stage to avoid being crushed.

"Ow!" She landed badly, twisting her ankle.

The Graydig shuffled closer to the stage. With every step, it seemed to grow bigger and more terrifying. It was feeding off their fear.

Tamzin leapt up and held up her hands, her ring glowing red.

"Idan *and goodness never fail,*
Ancient powers, send a gale."

Tamzin's ring burned, bright as a flame. A wind began to blow. The breeze whirled around Tamzin, lifting her braids, plastering her skirt against her legs. The wind picked up speed, turning into a gale that ripped the ivy off the wall, swirling it into in a cone shape, a spinning twister of vines. The ivy twister spun faster and faster, lifting high into the sky. It spun towards the hooded figure, flinging itself like a huge lasso around the Graydig, tightening around its cloak.

The hooded cloak collapsed into a crumpled heap and damp fingers of green fog drifted into the air. For a moment, Jenny thought that Tamzin's magic had worked. And then the fog thickened, turning into a cloud that whizzed in the air like a giant tornado.

The ivy leaves shrivelled and withered, like the ones on the trees by the sinkhole.

The Graydig's hooded figure loomed up, larger than ever, casting a deep shadow over the stage.

Jenny, still crouched on the ground, touched her bracelet and the spell flowed from her very soul.

"Mófǎ *triumphs over wrong,*
Ancient powers, give me a song."

Jenny felt the rush of magical energy flow into her. In a trance, she began to dance, turning one way and then the other way, following the ancient steps of her ancestor, the shaman. She was using every last ounce of her energy to concentrate and block out the chaos all around her.

The noise fell away. The chaos dimmed. Jenny opened her eyes and realised that she was facing the hooded Graydig under the great oak tree, one on one.

Jenny opened her mouth and the melody of the shaman's song flowed from her.

The Graydig started to cackle. Louder and louder, drowning out Jenny's song. "Stop trying. You're not strong enough to defeat me – not a puny, lonely girl like you!"

Jenny's bracelet glowed bright green. Her face tingled, and the bubbling pressure rose up her nose. There was a sudden lurch and then . . .

Jenny's spirit floated out of her body to hover above the stage and the Graydig. "NO!" she cried. "I need to be down there, not up here!" But up and up she floated still, into the sky, towards the clouds, the garden below shrinking the higher she rose. The grand old oak tree shrank too as she went back in time, decades flashing by in seconds. The Oaks was gone, and

in its place was an old
farmhouse, and then there
was nothing.

The oak tree grew younger and
younger until it was a slim sapling in
the middle of a lush green field. Four
young women in long robes were
standing together in the field, holding

hands around the oak sapling, singing.

Jenny's eyes widened as she recognised the tune. It was the folk song they'd learned in music class! The lyrics that the Spellcasters had rearranged and were planning to perform at the fair.

"Come with me to the great oak tree,
Come and sing and dance with me.
Together we are stronger by the great oak tree.
Together we stand, brave, bold and free."

A figure in a hooded cloak loomed above them. It was the Graydig. It cackled with glee, and puffs of green mist wafted from its cloak.

"*Come with me to the great oak tree, come and sing and dance with me . . .*" Each of the girls was wearing a necklace with a Celtic rune symbol hanging from the leather cord. The runes were glowing brightly. As the girls sang, beams of light shot out from their mouths, filling the air with magical sparkles.

There was a flash of light from the ley line, and the ground trembled and shook. A massive sinkhole appeared in the ground, in the exact same spot the sinkhole was in now.

The girls carried on singing. *"Together we are stronger by the great oak tree."* As their voices sang in unison, more light and magic poured out of their mouths. The light wound around the Graydig, pulling it down and trapping it. Eventually, the light pulled the Graydig into the sinkhole. The hooded figure screeched as it fell.

"Together we stand, brave, bold and free."

The sinkhole closed with a thump, sealing the Graydig deep inside. The girls' necklaces stopped glowing.

With a lurch, Jenny snapped back into her body and real time resumed. The Graydig was still standing in front of her, its eerie cackles echoing around.

Just like the Spellcasters, the four medieval girls had used magic handed down from their ancestors. Their magical powers grew stronger when they sang together.

Jenny ran away from the Graydig and gathered the Spellcasters together. "We need to sing together while we each channel the power of our ancestors, all at the same time. Working together will make our magic more powerful." Jenny looked at them all, her eyes shining.

"That's how the Graydig was defeated in the past. By four friends singing together, working their magic all at once. It's the only way."

CHAPTER TWELVE

The four girls climbed back on to the stage, facing the Graydig, with the oak tree behind them.

"Hold hands, everyone," shouted Jenny.

The Graydig loomed taller than ever, its shadow casting an impenetrable shade. "You will never defeat me! You

are just puny little children."

"Four girls defeated you hundreds of years ago," said Jenny. "And we'll do it again."

"Ah," sneered the Graydig. "But there is much more discord in the world today. I am more powerful now than I ever was before."

"Come on, Spellcasters," said Jenny, as the band joined hands. "Let's call the power of the ancients." She closed her eyes and they each cast a spell, asking their ancestors to help them defeat the evil Graydig.

The four talismans glowed brighter than Jenny had ever seen.

"*Come with me, to the great oak tree,*" Jenny sang loudly. The Spellcasters joined her.

"*Come and sing and dance with me.*
Together we are stronger by the great oak tree.
Together we stand, brave, bold and free."

Bright white light curled out of the girls' mouths as they sang, filling the air with magic.

The Graydig flew towards them with a threatening growl. But the girls' magic was too strong. It pushed the Graydig back. Thick green mist billowed from its cloak until the girls could hardly see each other.

Coughing and spluttering, the girls carried on singing. The light streaming from their jewellery dazzled the green mist, forcing it back.

Jenny's face and head were tingling, but she didn't stop singing. And then she felt the now-familiar lurch.

This time, as Jenny rose out of her body, she saw other glowing spirits gathering in the sky. The four medieval girls hovered above them, holding hands over the now much older great oak tree, joining in with the folk song.

Jenny floated further up. She saw a figure wearing the headdress of a cat from ancient Egypt, singing Maya's spell.

Next, she saw a woman in colourful silks, singing Ananya's spell.

Another figure, her braided hair

adorned with cowrie shells, was singing
Tamzin's spell.

Lastly, Jenny saw her own ancestor,
the Wu, with her trailing sleeves and
bone headdress.

Jenny smiled, filled with happiness.
Four ancestors, along with the medieval

Spellcroft girls, were standing with the Spellcasters to fight the evil spirit.

Jenny focused all her efforts on moving back into her body. And then she was back on the stage, Maya's hand in her left hand, Tamzin's hand in her right.

"Keep singing!" yelled Jenny. "Our ancestors are helping us!"

Time resumed and the Spellcasters sang on. The magical energy pouring out of their voices had tripled in strength and at last began to disperse the green smoke.

As the girls sang, their talisman jewellery glowed brighter and brighter, and magical light looped around the Graydig.

"You can't defeat me!" the hooded figure shrieked, twisting and turning, attempting to escape the grip of the magical light. It shouted and screeched, but its voice was losing power, fading to a shrill whisper.

Then, finally, the Graydig stopped twisting. It rose high into the air as if trying to get away from the Spellcasters. Up and up, past the clouds it soared, until it was a tiny dot in the sky.

But Jenny did not lose hope. She knew that their ancestors and the medieval girls were up there, in the spirit world, helping them. They were unstoppable while they all stood together.

With the last verse ringing out into the air, the Graydig came crashing down.

Down, down, down . . . and down it sank, into the sinkhole.

A streak of light flashed underground, on either side of the sinkhole.

That's the ley line! realised Jenny. She'd seen it before, but now she understood what it was.

With a teeth-juddering screech and another bright flash of light, the earth shifted. Clumps of crumbly soil pushed up like molehills, filling in the gap.

"You haven't seen the last of me . . ."

came the faint sound of the Graydig's voice.

Then the rocks shifted and groaned and the sinkhole closed, trapping the Graydig back in its lair. The ley line flashed again, the earth tremored for a final time, and two jagged boulders rolled forward to seal it in.

The girls stopped singing, looking at each other with relief.

"We did it," said Jenny.

Maya hopped off the stage and sank down on the grass, and the other girls followed.

They lay back, gazing up at the now-clear sky.

The mist disappeared and the sun came out from behind the clouds. A stunning rainbow appeared in the sky.

"When we put our powers together, we can achieve anything." Ananya grinned.

"Now can you wish away this mess?" asked Tamzin. The stalls looked like a giant had trampled all over them.

"I'll give it a go," said Ananya, and she conjured her magic with ease. Tables straightened up, torn coverings magically stitching themselves back together. The food stalls were once again laden with delicious dishes.

Tamzin held up her ring and cast a spell to heal the dead trees and the ivy. With the Graydig gone, her magic was more powerful; withered branches and leaves perked up, and fresh tendrils of ivy crept over the walls.

Ananya and Tamzin finished working their magic and stood back, satisfied. The fair looked even better than before.

"Girls!" Aunty Connie cried. "What's going on out here? I thought you were coming inside."

"Do you think she saw anything?" whispered Jenny to Ananya.

"Nah, she wouldn't have believed her eyes anyway," Ananya said, grinning.

They'd defeated the Graydig without anyone seeing them in action. Which, when Jenny thought about it, was just how she wanted it. It felt good to have a magical secret that only the Spellcasters shared.

"Aunty Connie," Jenny called. "The stinky mist has gone – tell everyone to come back outside."

Aunty Connie led the people back out of the centre and into the garden. With the sun now shining and the sky clear, more people began flowing into the garden from the street outside, lured by the smell of the delicious food stalls and the promise of live music.

Aunty Connie stepped back on to the stage with a pair of scissors. "I now declare the Spellcroft Fair open!"

The girls performed their song to rapturous applause and Jenny was sure the medieval girls were bopping along somewhere up in the spirit world.

They danced to the other bands till
Por Por called them over to their food
stall.

"Jenny, *bao-beh*! We have so much
leftover food. Come, you and your
friends must help finish."

"Wow – these look amazing!" Tamzin

grinned, taking a curry puff from Gong
Gong.

"Mmm, extra hot," said Ananya,
taking a bite. "My favourite."

Aunty Connie rushed over and
pointed out the people from the council.
Two of them were dancing to a rock

song, and a third was carrying a plate piled high with food from around the world.

"Guess what," said Aunty Connie, hopping up and down with excitement. "I've just delivered my petition to the council members, and it's not official yet, but one of the councilwomen said there were too many issues with the site. The shopping complex isn't going to go ahead. The Oaks has been saved!"

The Spellcasters high-fived.

Jenny's phone buzzed. "Hi, Jenny!" Mum and Dad crowded on to her screen.

"We watched the livestream," Mum

said. "It was quite erratic, kept cutting off for ages. But we caught your song in the end. Well done; it was fabulous!"

Jenny drew her friends in. "Guys, these are my parents."

"Good work, Spellcasters!" Dad put his thumbs up.

Mum clapped. "Well done, Jenny, Maya, Ananya and Tamzin. What a performance!"

Jenny turned to her friends and smiled. Finally, she wasn't the new girl any more. She had a best friend. Three of them, actually!

Jenny held out her hand and, one by one, her friends slapped their hands on top, their matching friendship bracelets glinting in the sun. Jenny knew they had loads more to learn about their magical powers – and she couldn't wait. Whatever came next, Jenny knew that the Spellcasters would face it together.

"Spellcasters for ever!" they said in unison.

The End

Spellcasters

THE ADVENTURE CONTINUES IN BOOK TWO:

POTION POWER

When a mysterious newcomer joins the Spellcroft community garden project, things start going wrong. Strange plants sprout all over town, a lake dries up and people fall ill. Could Tamzin's ancestral magic hold the key to restoring the balance of nature?